"You've ne

"Never." Jay's heart did a funny dance as he held the baby in his arms. He couldn't stop looking at Lacey. And she had the nerve to laugh at him.

"Sit down before you drop her. You look a little pale," Lacey said.

Jay sat, still clutching the tiny little girl in his arms. He smiled down at her, and she smiled back, her tiny nose scrunching up.

"Now aren't you something else." He spoke softly and the baby smiled again. "You're a little charmer. I think I'll buy you a pony."

"She wants a bay," Lacey said, still smiling. "Ready to go?"

He handed the baby over, still unsure with her in his arms. As he looked at Lacey, she was one more thing that he was suddenly unsure about.

Jay held the front door and let Lacey walk out first because he was afraid to walk next to her, afraid of what it might feel like to be close to her with a baby in her arms and a smile on her face.

Books by Brenda Minton

Love Inspired

Trusting Him
His Little Cowgirl
A Cowboy's Heart
The Cowboy Next Door

BRENDA MINTON

started creating stories to entertain herself during hour-long rides on the school bus. In high school she wrote romance novels to entertain her friends. The dream grew and so did her aspirations to become an author. She started with notebooks, handwritten manuscripts and characters that refused to go away until their stories were told. Eventually she put away the pen and paper and got down to business with the computer. The journey took a few years, with some encouragement and rejection along the way—as well as a lot of stubbornness on her part. In 2006, her dream to write for Steeple Hill Love Inspired came true.

Brenda lives in the rural Ozarks with her husband, three kids and an abundance of cats and dogs. She enjoys a chaotic life that she wouldn't trade for anything—except, on occasion, a beach house in Texas. You can stop by and visit at her Web site, www.brendaminton.net.

The Cowboy
Next Door
Brenda Minton

Steeple Hill®

Published by Steeple Hill Books™

STEEPLE HILL BOOKS

Steeple Hill®

Recycling programs
for this product may
not exist in your area.

ISBN-13: 978-0-373-87530-6
ISBN-10:   0-373-87530-4

THE COWBOY NEXT DOOR

Copyright © 2009 by Brenda Minton

Printed in U.S.A.

Truly my soul silently waits for God;
From Him comes my salvation.
—*Psalms* 62:1

This book is dedicated to my mom,
Rosetta (Kasiah) Cousins. (May 1937–November
1980). She taught me to dream and she encouraged
me to use my imagination. She put up with baby
birds and mice in the house, numerous wild kittens,
possums, ponies, goats and puppies. And to my
dad, Don Cousins, who is still excited by every
accomplishment. You taught me the value of hard
work, even when I didn't appreciate it. I love you.

And to the memory of Patsy Grayson,
encourager, friend, blessing.

Chapter One

"Lacey, when are you going to go out with me?" Bobby Fynn hollered from across the dining room of the Hash-It-Out Diner.

"Maybe next week," Lacey called back as she refilled an empty coffee cup, smiling at her customer, an older woman with curly black hair and a sweet smile.

"Come on, Lacey, you can't keep turning me down."

Lacey smiled and shook her head, because Bobby wasn't serious, and she wasn't interested.

"Ignore him," Marci, the hostess, whispered as Lacey walked past.

Lacey shot her friend a smile. "He doesn't bother me. I'll be back in a minute. I need to get a pitcher of water."

She hurried to the waitress station, set the glass coffeepot on the warming tray, and grabbed the pitcher of ice water. The cowbell over the door clanged, announcing the arrival of another customer. She hustled around the corner, pretending her feet weren't blistered and her back wasn't aching from the double shifts she'd worked for the last week.

If it wasn't for the perfect piece of land she wanted to buy…

Two strong hands grabbed her arms, stopping her mid-stride

and preventing a near collision. The pitcher of ice water she'd carried out of the waitress station sloshed, soaking her shirt. She looked up, muttering about clumsiness and met the dark gaze of Officer Jay Blackhorse.

Gorgeous, he was definitely gorgeous. Tall with black hair and brown eyes. All cowboy. All rugged and sure of himself. But not her type. He'd been back in Gibson, Missouri, for a month now, and she already had him figured out. He was too serious, not the kind of customer who chatted with a waitress, and she was fine with the knowledge that they weren't going to be best friends.

Several men called out, offering him a chair at their table, as Lacey moved out of his grasp. Not only was he the law, his family also raised cattle and horses. He hadn't lived in Gibson for the last seven or eight years, but he still fit in on so many levels that Lacey didn't know how he could do it all.

She was still trying to find something other than round holes for her square-peg self.

She was the girl from St. Louis who had showed up six years ago with a broken-down car, one hundred dollars and the dream of finding a new life.

Jay waved at the men who called out to him, but he didn't take them up on their offers to sit. Instead, he took hold of Lacey's arm and moved her toward the door.

"Lacey, I need to talk to you outside."

"Sure." Of course, not a problem.

She set the pitcher of ice water on a table and followed him to the door, trying hard not to remember her other life, the life that had included more than one trip in the back of a police car.

It would have been a waste of breath to tell Jay she wasn't that person any more. He didn't know her.

He didn't know what it had been like to grow up in her home, with a family that had fallen apart before she could walk. Jay had a mom who baked cookies and played the piano at church. Lacey's mom had brought home boyfriends for herself and her daughters.

Instead of protesting, Lacey shot Jay a disgusted look—as if it didn't matter—and exited the diner at his side. When they were both outside, she turned on him, pushing down her pain and reaching for the old Lacey, the one who knew how to handle these situations.

"What's this all about, Blackhorse? Is it 'humiliate the waitress day' and someone nominated me to get the prize?"

He shook his head and pointed to his car. "Sorry, Lacey, but I didn't know what else to do with her."

"Her?"

The back door of the patrol car opened.

Lacey watched the young woman step out with a tiny baby in her arms and a *so what* look on her face. Jay's strong hand gripped Lacey's arm, holding her tight as she drew in a deep breath and tried to focus. She pulled her arm free because she wasn't about to fall.

Or fall apart.

Even at twenty-two Corry still looked drugged-out, antsy and on the verge of running. Her dark eyes were still narrowed in anger—as if the world had done her wrong. The thrust of her chin told everyone she would do what she wanted, no matter whom it hurt.

Jay stood next to Lacey, his voice low. "She said she hitched a ride to Gibson and that she's your sister."

Lacey wanted to say that it wasn't true and that she didn't have a sister. She wanted to deny she knew the young woman with the dirty black hair and a baby in her arms.

The baby cried and Lacey made eye contact with Corry.

"She's my sister," Lacey said, avoiding Jay's gaze.

"Thanks for claiming me." Corry smacked her gum, the baby held loosely against her shoulder, little arms flailing. The loose strap of Corry's tank top slid down her shoulder, and her shorts were frayed.

Lacey sighed.

"I don't have to leave her here." Jay pulled sunglasses from his pocket and slid them on, covering melted-chocolate eyes. The uniform changed him from the cowboy that sat with the guys during lunch to someone in authority.

Lacey nodded because he did have to leave Corry. What else could he do? What was Lacey going to do? Deny her sister? The Samaritan had cared for the man on the side of the road, a man he didn't know. And Lacey *knew* Corry.

"She can stay. I'm off duty in thirty minutes."

"Do you have to make it sound like the worst thing in the world?" Corry handed Lacey the baby and turned to pick up the backpack that Jay had pulled from the trunk of his car.

Lacey looked at the infant. The baby, Corry's baby, was dressed in pink and without a single hair on her head. She was beautiful.

"Her name's Rachel." Corry tossed the information like it didn't matter. "I heard that in a Bible story at the mission we've been living in. We couldn't stay there, though. We need a real home."

A real home? The one-room apartment that Lacey rented from the owners of the Hash-It-Out was hardly a home fit for three.

She inhaled a deep breath of air that smelled like the grill inside the diner, and the lunch special of fried chicken. Corry and a baby. Family meant something. Lacey had learned that in Gibson, not in the home she grew up in. Now was the time to put it into practice. She could tell her sister to leave, or she could be the person who gave Corry a chance.

Like the people of Gibson had done for her.

But what if Corry ruined everything? Lacey tucked that fear away, all the while ignoring the imposing Officer Blackhorse in his blue-and-gray uniform, gun hanging at his side.

"You know, you two could help me," Corry tossed over her shoulder as she dug around in the back seat of the patrol car. "I haven't eaten since this morning. And then I get here and you aren't even glad to see me."

Continuous jabber. Lacey tuned it out, nodding in what she hoped were the appropriate places. She held Corry's baby close and took the car seat that Jay had pulled out of his car. His gaze caught and held hers for a moment, and his lips turned in a hesitant smile that shifted the smooth planes of his face. Jay with his perfect life and his perfect family.

She didn't want to think about what he thought when he looked at her and her sister.

"Need anything?" Jay took a step back, but he didn't turn away.

She shrugged off the old feelings of inadequacy and turned to face her sister. Corry shifted from foot to foot, hugging herself tight with arms that were too thin and scarred from track marks—evidence of her drug use.

"Lacey?" Jay hadn't moved away and she didn't know what to say.

Lacey Gould's dark, lined eyes were luminous with unshed tears. Jay hadn't expected that reaction from the waitress who always had a comeback. He held a grudging admiration for her because she never slowed down.

And he knew her secrets, just as he knew that her sister had prior arrests. Corry Gould had two drug convictions and one charge of prostitution. She was a repeat offender. A simple run through the state system was all it took to find out if a person had a criminal record. In Lacey's case, the Gibson police chief had filled him in. Jay hadn't been sure if it had been gossip or serious concern for his parents. They had spent a lot of time with Lacey Gould in his absence.

His parents hadn't appreciated his concern, though. They

knew all about Lacey's arrest record, and they knew who she was now. That was good enough for them.

He'd been a cop for too long to let it be good enough for him.

Lacey shifted next to him, the baby fussing.

She was slight in build, but not thin. Her brown eyes often flashed with humor and she had a mouth that smiled as much as it talked. He tried to ignore the dark hair, cut in a chunky style and highlighted with streaks of red.

For the moment her energy and feistiness were gone. He couldn't leave her like that.

"Lacey, I can take her to the station," Jay offered, knowing she wouldn't accept. She scraped leftovers from plates at the diner to feed stray cats; he doubted she would turn away her sister and that baby.

Corry moved closer to Lacey. The younger sister had the baby now, holding the infant in one arm and the dingy backpack in the other. Her eyes, blue, rather than Lacey's dark brown, shimmered with tears.

Lacey was motionless and silent, staring at her sister and the baby.

"I have to take the baby somewhere, Lace. The guy who dropped me off at the city limits was going south, way south. I don't have a way back to St. Louis."

"I'm not going to turn my back on you, Corry. But as long as you're here, you have to stay clean and stay out of trouble."

"If it helps, I checked her bag and she doesn't have anything on her." Jay could tell when Lacey bit down on her bottom lip and studied her sister that this information didn't really help.

He shrugged because he didn't know what else to do. The two sisters were eyeing one another, the baby was fussing and his radio squawked a call. He stepped away from the two women and answered the county dispatcher.

"Sorry, I have to run, but if you need anything—" he handed

Lacey a card with his cell phone number "—I'm just a phone call away."

"Thanks, Jay. We'll be fine." She took the card and shoved it into her pocket without looking at him.

"That's fine, but just in case." He shifted his attention to her sister. He had a strong feeling that Corry wasn't really here looking for a place to start over.

As he got into his patrol car and looked back, he saw Lacey standing on the sidewalk looking a little lost. He'd never seen that look on her face before, like she wasn't sure of her next move.

He brushed off the desire to go back. He knew he couldn't help her. Lacey was a force unto herself, independent and determined. He was pretty sure she didn't need him, and more than positive he didn't want to get involved.

Lacey watched Jay Blackhorse drive away before turning to face Corry again. The front door of the diner opened and Lacey's boss, Jolynn, stepped outside.

"Honey, if you need to take off early, go ahead. We can handle it for thirty minutes without you." Jolynn smiled at Corry.

Lacey wished she could do the same. She wished that seeing her sister here didn't make her feel as if her life in Gibson was in danger.

"I can stay." Lacey picked up the backpack that Corry had tossed on the ground.

"No, honey, I insist. Go home." Jolynn patted her arm. "Take your sister on up to your place and get her settled."

Lacey closed her eyes and counted to ten. She could do this. "Okay, thank you. I'll grab my purse. But if you need…"

"We don't need. You're here too much as it is. It won't hurt you to go home a few minutes early."

Lacey stepped back inside the cool, air-conditioned diner

with Jolynn, and pretended people weren't staring, that they weren't whispering and looking out the window at her sister.

She pretended it didn't bother her. But it did. It bothered her to suddenly become the outsider again, after working so hard to gain acceptance. It bothered her that Jay Blackhorse never looked at her as though she belonged.

Jolynn gave her a light hug when she walked her to the door. "You're a survivor, Lacey, and you'll make it through this. God didn't make a mistake, bringing that young woman to you."

Lacey nodded, but she couldn't speak. Jolynn smiled and opened the door for her. Lacey walked out into the hot July day. Corry had taken a seat on the bench and she stood up.

"Ready?" Lacey picked up her sister's bag.

"Where's your car?"

"I walk to work."

"We have to walk?"

Lacey took off, letting Corry follow along behind her. Her sister mumbled and the baby whimpered in the infant seat. Lacey glanced back, the backpack and diaper bag slung over her shoulder, at her sister who carried the infant seat with the baby.

As they walked up the long driveway to the carriage-house apartment Lacey had lived in for over six years, Corry mumbled a little louder.

Lacey opened the door to her apartment and motioned her sister inside. The one room with a separate bathroom and a walk-in closet was less than five hundred square feet. Corry looked around, clearly not impressed.

"You've been living in a closet." Corry smirked. "And I thought you were living on Walton's Mountain."

Ignore it. Let it go. Push the old Lacey aside. "I think you should feed the baby."

"Ya think? So now you're a baby expert."

The old Lacey really wanted to speak up and say something mean. The new Lacey smiled. "I'm not an expert."

Corry had done nothing but growl since they'd left the diner. Obviously she needed a fix. And she wasn't going to get one.

"Is there another room?"

"No, there isn't. We'll make do here until I can get something else." Lacey looked around the studio apartment that had been her home since she'd arrived in Gibson.

The home she would have to give up if Corry stayed in Gibson. Starting over again didn't feel good. The baby whimpered. A six-week-old child, dependent on the adults in her life to make good choices for her.

Starting over for a baby. Lacey could do that. She would somehow make it work. She would do her best to help Corry, because that meant the baby had a chance.

Corry tossed her backpack into a corner of the room and dumped the baby, crying and working her fist in her mouth, onto the hide-a-bed that Lacey hadn't put up that morning.

Lacey lifted the baby to her shoulder and rubbed the tiny back until she quieted. Corry had walked to the small kitchen area and was rummaging through the cabinets.

"You know, Corry, since you're here, wanting a place to live, maybe you should try being nice."

"I am being nice." Corry turned from the cabinets and flashed a smile that didn't reach her eyes. "And your boyfriend is cute."

"He isn't my boyfriend." Lacey walked across the room, the baby snuggling against her shoulder. She couldn't let her sister bait her. She couldn't let her mind go in that direction, with Jay Blackhorse as the hero that saved the day. "Corry, if you're going to be here, there are a few rules."

"Rules? I'm not fourteen anymore."

"No, you're not fourteen, but this is my house and my life that you've invaded."

Lacey closed her eyes and tucked the head of the baby against her chin, soft and safe. Be fair, she told herself. "I'm sorry, Corry, I know you need a place for the baby."

"I need a place for myself, too."

"I know that, and I'm willing to help. But I have to know that you're going to stay clean. You can't play your games in Gibson."

Corry turned, her elfin chin tilted and her eyes flashing anger. "You think you're so good, don't you, Lacey? You came to a small town where you pretend to be someone you're not, and suddenly you're too good for your family. You're afraid that I'm going to embarrass you."

"I'm not too good for my family. And it isn't about being embarrassed." It was about protecting herself, and the people she cared about.

It was about not being hurt or used again. And it was about keeping her life in order. She had left chaos behind when she left St. Louis.

"You haven't been home in three years." Corry shot the accusation at her, eyes narrowed.

No, Lacey hadn't been home. That accusation didn't hurt as much as the one about her pretending to be someone she wasn't.

Maybe because she hoped if she pretended long enough, she would actually become the person she'd always believed she could be. She wouldn't be the girl in the back of a patrol car, lights flashing and life crumbling. She wouldn't be the young woman at the back of a large church, wondering why she couldn't be loved without it hurting.

She wouldn't be invisible.

Lacey shifted the fussing baby to one side and grabbed the backpack and searched for something to feed an infant. She found one bottle and a half-empty can of powdered formula.

"Feed your daughter, Corry."

"Admit you're no better than me." Corry took the bottle and the formula, but she didn't turn away.

"I'm not better than you." Lacey swayed with the baby held against her. She wasn't better than Corry, because just a few short years ago, she had been Corry.

But for the grace of God…

Her life had changed. She walked to the window and looked out at the quiet street lined with older homes centered on big, tree-shaded lawns. A quiet street with little traffic and neighbors that cared.

"Here's her bottle." Corry shoved the bottle at Lacey. "And since the bed is already out, I'm taking a nap."

Lacey nodded, and then she realized what had just happened. Corry was already working her. Lacey slid the bottle into the mouth of the hungry infant and moved between her sister and the bed.

"No, you're not going to sleep. That's rule number one if you're going to stay. You're not going to sleep while I work, take care of the baby and feed you. I have to move to make this possible, so you're going to have to help me out a little. I'll have to find a place, and then we'll have to pack."

Corry was already shaking her head. "I didn't say you have to move, so I'm not packing a thing."

Twenty-some years of battling and losing.

"You're going to feed Rachel." Lacey held the baby out to her reluctant sister.

Corry took the baby, but her gaze shifted to the bed, the blankets pulled up to cover the pillows. For a moment Lacey almost caved. She nearly told her sister she could sleep, because she could see in Corry's eyes that she probably hadn't slept in a long time.

"Fine." Corry sat down in the overstuffed chair that Jolynn had given Lacey when she'd moved into the carriage-house apartment behind the main house.

"I need to run down to the grocery store." Lacey grabbed her purse. "When I get back, I'll cook dinner. You can do the dishes."

"They have a grocery store in this town?" Corry's question drew Lacey out of thoughts that had turned toward how she'd miss this place, her first home in Gibson.

"Yes, they have a store. Do you need something?"

"Cig…"

"No, you won't smoke in my house or around Rachel."

"Fine. Get me some chocolate."

Lacey stopped at the door. "I'm going to get formula and diapers for the baby. I'll think about the chocolate."

As she walked out the door, Lacey took a deep breath. She couldn't do this. She stopped next to her car and tried to think of what she couldn't do. The list was long. She couldn't deal with her sister, or moving, or starting over again.

But she couldn't mistreat Corry.

If she was going to have faith, and if she was ever going to show Corry that God had changed her life, then she had to be the person she claimed to be. She had to do more than talk about being a Christian.

She shoved her keys back into her purse and walked down the driveway. A memory flashed into her mind, ruining what should have been a relaxing walk. Jay's face, looking at her and her sister as if the two were the same person.

Chapter Two

Jay finished his last report, on the accident he'd worked after leaving Lacey's sister at the diner. He signed his name and walked into his boss's office. Chief Johnson looked it over and slid it into the tray on his desk.

"Do you think the sister is going to cause problems?" Chief Johnson pulled off his glasses and rubbed the bridge of his nose.

"Of course she will."

"Why? Because she has a record? She could be like Lacey, really looking for a place to start over."

"I don't know that much about Lacey. But I'm pretty sure about her sister."

"Okay, then. Make sure you patrol past Lacey's place a few times every shift. I'll let the other guys know." The Chief put his glasses back on. "I guess you've got more work to do when you get home?"

"It's Wednesday and Dad schedules his surgeries for today. I've got to get home and feed."

"Tomorrow's your day off. I'll see you Friday."

"Friday." Jay nodded and walked out, fishing his keys out of his pocket as he walked.

He had to stop by the feed store on his way home, for the fly spray they'd ordered for him. At least he didn't have to worry about dinner.

His mom always cooked dinner for him on Wednesdays. She liked having him home again, especially with his brother and sister so far away. His sister lived in Georgia with her husband and new baby. His brother was in the navy.

It should have been an easy day to walk off the job, but it wasn't. As he climbed into his truck he was still remembering the look on Lacey's face when she watched her sister get out of the back of his car.

He knew what it was like to have everything change in just a moment. Life happened that way. A person could feel like they have it all under control, everything planned, and then suddenly, a complete change of plans.

A year ago he really had thought that by now he'd be married and living in his new home with a wife and maybe a baby of his own on the way.

Instead he was back in Gibson and Cindy was on her way to California. She'd been smarter than him; she'd realized three years of dating didn't equal love. And he was still living in the past, in love with a memory.

As he passed the store, he saw his mom's car parked at an angle, between the lines and a little too far back into the street. He smiled, because that was his mom. She lived her life inside the lines, but couldn't drive or park between them.

Other than the parking problem, they were a lot alike.

He drove to the end of the block, then decided to go back. She typically wasn't in town this time of day. Something must have gone wrong with dinner. He smiled because something usually did go wrong.

He parked in front of the store and reached for the truck-door handle. He could see his mom inside; she was talking to Lacey Gould. He let go of the door handle and sat back to wait.

He sat in the truck for five minutes. His mom finally approached the cash register at the single counter in the store. She paid, talked to the cashier for a minute and then walked out the door. Lacey was right behind her.

Talk about a day going south in a hurry.

"Jay, you remember Lacey." Wilma Blackhorse turned a little pink. "Of course you do, you saw her this afternoon."

"Mom, we've met before." He had lived in Springfield, not Canada. He'd just never really had a reason to talk to Lacey.

Until today.

"Of course you have." His mom handed him her groceries and then leaned into the truck, resting her arms on the open window. "Well, I just rented her your grandparents' old house. And since you have tomorrow off, I told her you would help them move."

"That really isn't necessary." Lacey, dark hair framing her face and brown eyes seeking his, moved a little closer to his truck. "I can move myself."

"Of course you can't. What are you going to do, put everything in the back of your car?" Wilma shook her head and then looked at Jay again.

Lacey started to protest, and Jay had a few protests of his own. He didn't need trouble living just down the road from them. His mom had no idea what kind of person Corry Gould was.

Not that it would have stopped her.

He reached for another protest, one that didn't cast stones.

"Mom, we're fixing that house up for Chad." Jay's brother. And one summer, a long time ago, it had been Jamie's dream home. For one summer.

It had been a lifetime ago, and yet he still held on to dreams of forever and promises whispered on a summer night. His mom had brought Jamie and her family to Gibson, and changed all of their lives forever.

"Oh, Jay, Chad won't be out of the navy for three years. If he even gets out of the navy. You know he wants to make it a career." She patted his arm. "And you're building a house, so you don't need it."

He opened his mouth with more objections, but his mom's eyes narrowed and she gave a short shake of her head. Jay smiled past her.

Lacey, street-smart and somehow shy. And he didn't want to like her. He didn't want to see vulnerability in her eyes.

"I'll be over at about nine in the morning." He didn't sigh. "I'll bring a stock trailer."

"I don't want you to have to spend your day moving me."

He started his truck. "It won't be a problem. See you in the morning."

"Don't forget dinner tonight," his mom reminded.

"You don't have to cook for me. I could pick something up at the diner."

"I have a roast in the Crock-Pot."

That was about the worst news he'd heard all day. He shot a look past her and Lacey smiled, her dark eyes twinkling a little.

"A roast." He nodded. "That sounds good. Lacey, maybe you all could join us for dinner."

"Oh, I can't. I have to get home and pack."

He tipped his hat at her and gave her props for a quick escape. She'd obviously had his mother's roast before.

"Thanks, Jay." Lacey Gould backed away, still watching him, as if she wanted something more from him. He didn't have more to give.

"See you at home, honey." His mom patted his arm.

"Mom…"

His mom hurried away, leaving him with the groceries and

words of caution he had wanted to offer her. She must have known what he had to say. And she would have called him cynical and told him to give Lacey Gould and her sister a chance.

Lacey woke up early the next morning to soft gray light through the open window and the song of a meadowlark greeting the day. She rolled over on the air mattress she'd slept on and listened to unfamiliar sounds that blended with the familiar.

A rustle and then a soft cry. She sat up, brushing a hand through her hair and then rubbing sleep from her eyes. She waited a minute, blinking away the fuzzy feeling. The baby cried again.

"Corry, wake up." Lacey pushed herself up off the mattress and walked to the hide-a-bed. Corry's face was covered with the blanket and she slept curled fetus-style on her side.

"Come on, moving day."

Corry mumbled and pulled the pillow over her head.

Lacey stepped away from the bed and reached into the bassinet for the pacifier to quiet the baby. Rachel's eyes opened and she sucked hard on the binky. Lacey kissed the baby's soft little cheek and smiled.

"I'll get your bottle."

And then she'd finish packing. She side-stepped boxes as she walked to the kitchen. Nearly everything was packed. It hadn't taken long. Six years and she'd accumulated very little. She had books, a few pictures and some dust bunnies. She wouldn't take those with her.

Memories. She had plenty of memories. She'd found a picture of herself and Bailey at Bailey's wedding, and a note from Bailey's father's funeral last year.

She'd lived a real life in this apartment. In this apartment she had learned to pray. She had cooked dinner for friends. She had let go of love. She had learned to trust herself. Dating Lance had taught her lessons in trusting someone else. And when not to trust.

The baby was crying for real. Lacey filled the bottle and set it in a cup to run hot water over it. The bed squeaked. She turned and Corry was sitting up, looking sleepy and younger than her twenty-two years.

Life hadn't really been fair. Lacey reminded herself that her sister deserved a chance. Corry deserved for someone to believe in her.

Lacey remembered life in that bug-infested apartment that had been her last home in St. Louis. She closed her eyes and let the bad memories of her mother and nights cowering in a closet with Corry slide off, like they didn't matter.

She picked up the bottle and turned off the water. The dribble of formula she squeezed onto her wrist was warm. She took the bottle back to Corry and then lifted the baby out of the bassinet.

"Can you feed her while I finish packing?" Lacey kissed her niece and then lowered her into Corry's waiting arms.

Corry stared down at the infant, and then back at Lacey. "You make it look so easy."

"It isn't easy, Corry."

"I thought it would be. I thought I'd just feed her and she'd sleep, and stuff. I didn't want to give her away to someone I didn't know."

Lacey looked away from the baby and from more memories.

"I need to pack."

"I'm sorry, Lacey."

"Don't worry about it." Lacey grabbed clothes out of her dresser. "I'm going to take a shower while you feed her. You need to make sure you're up and around before Jay gets here."

When Lacey walked out of the bathroom, he was standing by the door, a cowboy in jeans, a T-shirt and a ball cap covering his dark hair. He nodded and moved away from the door. In the small confines of her apartment she realized how tall he was, towering over her, making her feel smaller than her five-feet-five height.

"Oh, you're earlier than I expected."

"I thought it would be best if we got most of it done before it gets hot."

"I don't have a lot. It won't take long." She looked around and so did Jay. This was her life, all twenty-eight years packed into a studio apartment.

"We should be able to get it all in the stock trailer and the back of my truck."

"Do you want a cup of coffee first? I still have a few things to pack."

"No coffee for me. I'll start carrying boxes out."

Lacey pointed to the boxes that she'd packed the night before. And she let him go, because he was Jay Blackhorse and he wasn't going to sit and have a cup of coffee with her. And she was okay with that.

Her six-month relationship with Lance Carmichael had taught her a lot. He had taught her not to open her heart up, not to share. She would never forget that last night, their last date.

I can't handle this. It's too much reality. His words echoed in her mind, taunting her, making a joke of her dreams.

"Are there any breakables in the boxes?" Jay had crossed the room.

Lacey turned from pouring herself a cup of coffee. He stood in front of the boxes, tall and suntanned, graceful for his size. He was all country, right down to the worn boots and cracked leather belt.

He turned and she smiled, because he wore a tan-and-brown beaded necklace that didn't fit what she knew about Jay Black-horse. Not that she knew much. Or would ever know much.

Funny, she wanted to know more. Maybe because he was city and country, Aeropostale and Wrangler. Maybe it was the wounded look in his eyes, brief flashes that she caught from time to time, before he shut it down and turned on that country-boy smile.

"I've marked the ones that are fragile," she answered, and then grabbed an empty box to pack the stuff in the kitchen that she hadn't gotten to the night before.

Jay picked up a box and walked out the front door, pushing it closed behind him. And Corry whistled. Lacey shot her sister a warning look and then turned to the cabinet of canned goods and boxes of cereal. She agreed with the whistle.

Two hours later Lacey followed behind Jay's truck and the stock trailer that contained her life. Corry had stayed behind. And that had been fine with Lacey. She didn't need her sister underfoot, and the baby would be better in an empty apartment than out in the sun while they unloaded furniture and boxes.

From visits with Jay's mom, Lacey had seen the farmhouse where Jay's grandparents had lived. But as she pulled up, it changed and it became her home. She swallowed a real lump in her throat as she parked next to the house and got out of her car.

The lawn was a little overgrown and the flower gardens were out of control, but roses climbed the posts at the corner of the porch and wisteria wound around a trellis at one side of the covered porch.

Her house.

Jay got out of his truck and joined her. "It isn't much."

"It's a house," she whispered, knowing he wouldn't understand. She could look down the road and see the large brick house he'd grown up in. It had five bedrooms and the living room walls were covered with pictures of the children and the new grandchild that Wilma Blackhorse didn't get to see enough of.

"Yes, it's a house." He kind of shrugged. He didn't get it.

"I've never lived in a house." She bit down on her bottom

lip, because that was more than she'd wanted to share, more than she wanted him to know about her.

"I see." He looked down at her, his smile softer than before. "You grew up in St. Louis, right?"

"Yes."

"I guess moving to Gibson was a big change?"

"It was." She walked to the back of his truck. "I want to thank you for this place, Jay. I know that you don't want me here…"

He raised a hand and shook his head. "This isn't my decision. But I don't have anything against you being here."

She let it go, but she could have argued. Of course he minded her being there. She could see it in his eyes, the way he watched her. He didn't want her anywhere near his family farm.

Jay followed Lacey up the back steps of the house and into the big kitchen that his grandmother had spent so much time in. The room was pale green and the cabinets were white. His mom had painted it a few years ago to brighten it up.

But it still smelled like his grandmother, like cantaloupe and vine-ripened tomatoes. He almost expected her to be standing at the stove, taking out a fresh batch of cookies.

The memory brought a smile he hadn't expected. It had been a long time since his grandmother's image had been the one that he envisioned in this house. It took him by surprise, that it wasn't Jamie he thought of in this house, the way he'd thought of her for nine years. He put the box down and realized that Lacey was watching him.

"Good memories?" she asked, curiosity in brown eyes that narrowed to study his face.

"Yes, good memories. My grandmother was a great cook." He didn't say, "unlike Mom."

"Oh, I see."

"I guess you probably do. My mom tries too hard to be

creative. She always ends up adding the wrong seasoning, the wrong spices. You know she puts cinnamon and curry on her roast, right?"

Lacey nodded. She was opening cabinets and peeking in the pantry. She turned, her smile lighting her face and settling in her eyes. Over a house.

"I love your mom." Lacey opened the box she'd carried in. "I want to be like her someday."

She turned a little pink and he didn't say anything.

"I want to have a garden and can tomatoes in the fall," she explained, still pink, and it wasn't what he wanted to hear.

He didn't want to hear her dreams, or what she thought about life. He didn't want to get pulled into her world. He wanted to live his life here, in Gibson, and he didn't want it to be complicated.

Past to present, Lacey Gould was complicated.

And she thought he was perfect. He could see it in her eyes, the way she looked at him, at his home and his family. She had some crazy idea that if a person was a Blackhorse, they skipped through life without problems, or without making mistakes.

"It's a little late for a garden this year." He started to turn away, but the contents of the box she was unpacking pulled him back. "Dogs?"

"What?"

"You like dogs."

"I like to collect them." She took a porcelain shepherd out of the box and dusted it with her shirt.

"How many more do you have?" He glanced into the box.

"Dozens."

"Okay, I have to ask, why dogs?" ·

She looked up at him, her head cocked a little to the side and a veil of dark brown hair falling forward to cover one cheek.

"Dogs are cute." She smiled, and he knew that was all he'd get from her.

He didn't really want more.

Dogs are cute. As Jay walked through the front door of his house the next morning, he had a hard time believing that Lacey could be right about dogs. He looked down at his bloodhound and shook his head. Dogs weren't cute. Dogs chewed up a guy's favorite shoes. Dogs slobbered and chewed on the leg of a chair.

"You're a pain in my neck." He ignored the sad look on the dog's face. "You have no idea how much I liked those shoes. And Mom is going to kill you for what you did to that chair."

Pete whined and rested his head on his paws. Jay picked up the leather tennis shoe and pointed it at the dog. Pete buried his slobbery face between his paws and Jay couldn't help but smile.

"Crazy mutt." Jay dropped the shoe. "So I guess I keep you and buy new shoes. Someday, buddy, someday it'll be one shoe too many. You're too old for this kind of behavior."

The dog's ears perked. Jay walked to the window and looked out. A truck was pulling away from the house at the end of the dirt lane. Two days after the fact and he remembered what the Chief had told him: keep an eye on things at Lacey's. Well, now it would be easy, because Lacey was next door.

He turned and pointed toward the back door. Pete stood up, like standing took a lot of effort, and lumbered to the door. "Outside today, my friend. Enjoy the wading pool, and don't chew up the lawn furniture."

One last look back and Pete went out the door, his sad eyes pleading with Jay for a reprieve. "Not today, Pete."

Jay walked across his yard, his attention on the house not far from his. A five-acre section of pasture separated them. He could see Lacey standing in the yard, pulling on the cord of a push mower.

He glanced at his watch. He had time before he had to head to work. Pushing aside his better sense, he headed down the road to see if she needed help.

"Good morning, neighbor." She stopped pulling and smiled when he walked up. "Would you like a cup of coffee?"

"No, thanks." He moved a little closer. "Do you want me to start it for you?"

"If you can. I've been pulling on that thing for five minutes."

"Does it have gas in it?"

She bit down on her bottom lip and her hands slid into her pockets. "I didn't check."

He would have laughed, but she already looked devastated. Mowing the lawn was probably a big part of the having-a-house adventure. He wouldn't tease her. He also wouldn't burst her bubble by telling her it wouldn't stay fun for long.

"Do you have a gas can?"

"By the porch. Cody brought it. I just figured the mower was full." She went to get the can of gas. Cody was a good guy to bring it. Jay liked the husband of one of his childhood friends, Bailey Cross.

Jay opened the gas cap, pushed the machine and shook his head. "No gas. He probably filled the gas can on the way over, so you'd have it."

"Of course." She had the gas can and he took it from her to fill the tank.

"I can mow it for you."

"No, I want to do it. Remember, I've never had a lawn."

The front door opened. Lacey's sister stepped out with the baby in her arms. The child was crying, her arms flailing the air. Corry shot a look in his direction. He tried not to notice the eyes that were rimmed with dark circles, or the way perspiration beaded across her pale face. He looked away.

"She won't stop crying." Corry pushed the baby into Lacey's arms.

"Did you burp her?" Lacey lifted the infant to her shoulder. "Corry, you have to take care of her. She's your daughter. You're all she has."

"I don't want to be all she has. How can I take care of her?"

"The same way thousands of moms take care of their children. You have to use a little common sense." Lacey made it look easy, leaning to kiss the baby's cheek, talking in quiet whispers that soothed the little girl.

He could have disagreed with Lacey. Not all moms knew how to take care of children. He'd been a police officer for five years. He'd seen a lot.

"I should go. I have to work today, but I wanted to make sure you have everything you need." He told himself he wasn't running from something uncomfortable.

"We're good." Lacey looked down at the baby. "Jay, thanks for this place."

"It needed to be rented." He shrugged it off. "But you're welcome."

"Hey, wait a minute." Corry moved forward, her thin arms crossed in front of her, hugging herself tight. "Aren't you going to tell him about the stove?"

Lacey smiled. "It isn't a big deal. I can fix it."

"Fix what?"

"One of the knobs is broken. I have to go to Springfield tonight. I can pick one up."

"What are you going to Springfield for?" Corry pushed herself into the conversation.

"None of your business." Lacey snuggled the baby and avoided looking at either of them. And Jay couldn't help but be curious. It was a hazard of his job. What was she up to?

"I can fix the stove, Lacey," he offered.

"Jay, I don't want you to think you have to run over here and fix every little thing that goes wrong. I'm pretty self-sufficient. I can even change my own lightbulbs."

"I'm sure you can." He looked at his watch. "Tell you what. You pick up the knob. I'll have my dad come over and fix it tomorrow."

That simplified everything. It meant he stayed out of her business. And she didn't feel like he was taking care of her.

"Good." She smiled her typical Lacey smile, full of optimism.

He had to take that thought back. Her sister showing up in town had emptied her of that glass-half-full attitude. Maybe her cheerful attitude did have limits.

"Do you want to see if the mower will start now?" He recapped the gas can and set it on the ground next to the mower. Lacey still held the baby.

"No, I have to get ready for work now."

"See you at the diner." He tipped his hat and escaped.

When he glanced back over his shoulder, they were walking back into the house and he wondered if Lacey would survive her sister being in her life.

And if he would survive the two of them in his.

Chapter Three

"I can't stay out here all day, alone." Corry paced through the sunlit living room of the farmhouse, plopping down on the overstuffed floral sofa that Lacey had bought used the previous day.

Lacey turned back to the window and watched as Jay made his way down the road to the home he'd grown up in. A perfect house for a perfect life.

For a while he'd even had a perfect girlfriend, Cindy, a law student and daughter of a doctor. The perfect match. Or maybe not. He was back at home, and Cindy was off to California pursuing her career. Lacey knew all of this through the rumor mill, which worked better than any small-town paper.

And the other thing they said was that it was all because of Jamie. But no one really talked about who Jamie was and what she meant to Jay Blackhorse.

"Come on, Lace, stop ignoring me." Corry, petulant and high-strung. Lacey sighed and turned back around.

"You'll have to stay here. I have to work, and I can't entertain you."

"I'll go to town with you."

"No, you're not going with me."

"Why not?" Corry plopped down on the sofa and put her feet up on the coffee table.

"Because I said so." Lacey rubbed a hand across her face. "This is not what I want to do every day, Corry. I don't want to raise you. You're a grown woman and a mother. If you're going to be bored, we'll find a sitter for Rachel and you can get a job."

Corry frowned and drew her legs up under her. The baby slept in the bassinet someone from church had donated to their new home. They both looked at the lace-covered basket.

"You know I can't work," she whispered, for a moment looking vulnerable.

"You stay home with the baby, Corry. Be a good mom and let me worry about working."

"I'm not worried about it."

Of course she wasn't. "Fine, then you can be responsible for cooking dinner."

"I can't cook. Well, maybe mac-n-cheese or sandwiches. Not much else."

"You can learn. I have cookbooks."

At the word *cookbook* she saw Corry's eyes glaze over, and the younger woman looked away.

"I want to call my friends and let them know where I am." Corry plucked at the fabric on the couch. "They'll be wondering what happened to me."

Lacey shook her head, fighting the sliver of fear that snaked into her belly when she thought about the kind of friends that Corry had. She didn't want that old life invading Gibson.

"You can't drag the old in with the new, Corry."

"Just because you walked away from everyone doesn't mean that I have to."

"I didn't walk away, I started over."

"I don't see how you can like it here."

Lacey stood up but didn't answer. She picked up her cell

phone and slipped it into her pocket, a way to let Corry know that she meant it when she said her sister couldn't contact people from her past.

"I'll be home by four o'clock. But after dinner, I have to go to Springfield for a few hours."

"Fine, have fun. Don't worry about me, stuck out here, alone, nothing to do."

"I won't."

Lacey grabbed the backpack off the hook on the wall and walked out the front door, letting it bang shut behind her. She heaved the backpack over her shoulder and glanced back, seeing Corry on the sofa, watching.

She couldn't tell Corry about the classes in Springfield, or what they meant to her. Corry wouldn't understand. Lacey was one month away from finishing high school. She would finally have a piece of paper to show that she had accomplished her goal.

As soon as the GED certificate was in her hands, she wanted to enroll in college. She wanted to be a teacher.

She wanted to help children who, like Corry, had never had a chance. Maybe if those children had someone to believe in them, their lives would take different paths than the path her sister had taken.

It was after ten o'clock Friday night when Jay saw headlights easing down the long drive to the old farmhouse that Lacey had rented. He dropped his book and went to the window.

"Who is it?" His mom turned down the volume on the news program she was watching.

"I'm not sure. Someone pulling into Lacey's."

Lacey's house was dark.

"You should go check on them. They don't have a phone yet." His mom had joined him at the window. She peered out into the dark night. Clouds covered the full moon but Jay could see stars to the south.

"Mom, I think they can take care of themselves." He shrugged off his own curiosity. "I'm not her keeper."

"You're also a nice guy. Don't try to pretend you're not." His mom gave him the mom look. "Jay, she's a sweet girl and she's worked hard to change her life."

"I'm sure she has. But I also don't think you can take in every stray that comes along."

"Okay, fine." She peered out the window again and then shrugged as if she didn't care.

"If it makes you happy, I'll go check on her. But I have a feeling she isn't going to appreciate it."

"Maybe not, but I will." She smiled at him, and he knew he'd lost the battle.

He grabbed a flashlight and his sidearm, sliding it into the holster he hadn't removed when he'd walked through the door thirty minutes earlier.

Pete woofed from the dog bed near the fireplace. The dog didn't bother getting up. He was retired from the police force and usually didn't care who did what.

Jay walked out the door and headed across a field bathed in silver light as the clouds floated overhead. Pete woofed again and he heard the dog door flap as the lazy animal ran to catch up with him. Obviously Pete had decided the action was worth getting up for. Five years of sniffing drugs and searching for lost kids, and now he spent most of his time sniffing rabbit trails and chewing up perfectly good shoes.

A shadow lingered in the front yard of the old farmhouse. Pete lumbered to Jay's side, growling a low warning. Jay's hand went to his sidearm and he walked more carefully, deliberately keeping an eye on the form that had stilled when the dog barked.

Pete took off, his long legs pounding and his jaws flapping.

The person in the yard ran for the car and was scrambling onto the hood. The outdoor security light had been shot out by kids nearly a year earlier. As clouds covered the moon, Jay thought about the mistake of not getting that light fixed.

"Who's there?" He recognized the trembling voice.

"Pete, down." The dog immediately obeyed Jay's command. He walked through the gate and crossed the lawn to find Lacey cowering on the hood of her own car. He should have recognized the headlights of her Chevy.

"Where in the world did he come from?" She didn't move to climb down from the car. He almost laughed, but she had books and she might throw them.

"He's mine."

"Do you always sic him on people when they come home at night?"

He held a hand out and she refused the offer. Lacey Gould, afraid? How did he process that information? She always seemed a little like David, confronting the world with five stones and a lot of faith.

And she collected dogs. Of course, not real ones.

"I didn't know it was you. I saw a car pulling up to a dark house, late."

She grasped the books and shot him a "stupid male" look. "So, I can't come home late?"

"You were in Springfield this late?"

"Do you interrogate all of your renters?"

"No, I don't interrogate all of them. It was a question, Lacey. You were going to Springfield after work. It's late. We saw headlights down here and we were worried. Mom was worried."

Her shoulders slumped. "I have to get inside. I have the breakfast shift and I have to be at work at five in the morning."

"Let me help you down."

"Jay, do me a favor, grab your dog."

"He won't hurt you."

"He's huge and he has big teeth."

"You're afraid of dogs." More information to process. He reached for Pete's collar. "What about that dog collection of yours?"

He shouldn't have asked. Asking meant he wanted to know something about her, something that didn't quite make sense. He wanted to deny that she was a mystery to solve.

He definitely didn't want to get involved.

"I love collecting dogs." She stared at Pete. "The kind without teeth."

"Toy ones." He smiled and she glared.

"Don't tell anyone. How embarrassing would it be if everyone knew?"

"People can be afraid of dogs, Lacey."

"It's a ridiculous fear. Some dogs bite."

"Pete doesn't bite."

She smiled. "But if he did, he'd take a big bite."

"He chews on shoes, but he barely chews his own dog food."

"You chew it for him?"

"Now that's disgusting."

She slid down from the hood of the car, but stayed on the other side of the vehicle. "I need to get some sleep. Thank you for checking on us."

He nodded and in the sliver of moonlight that filtered through a break in the clouds he read the book in her hand. *Algebra 2.* She hugged it tight to her chest.

"You don't have to know all of my secrets, Jay. At least you know I wasn't in town and up to no good."

"I never thought that." But hadn't he wondered? When she'd said she was going to Springfield tonight, hadn't he suspected something?

"You did. And that's fine."

She turned and walked away. He held on to Pete's collar and watched her go. Her back was straight and her step was less than bouncy.

Pete pulled, trying to go after her. Jay almost agreed with the dog, but decided against it. One thing he didn't need was more information about Lacey Gould.

Saturday mid-morning and the diner was full. Every table. Lacey hurried to the table where the Golden Girls were having Saturday brunch. Not that the Hash-It-Out served brunch; for Gibson, that meant a late breakfast if Jolynn still had biscuits left.

"Lacey, honey, how are you doing?" Elsbeth Jenkins pointed to her coffee cup. She could chat as much as anyone, and Lacey knew the older lady really did care. But Elsbeth did have her priorities. Coffee first.

"I'm doing fine, Miss Jenkins." Lacey poured the cup of coffee and handed her a few more creamers. "Is there anything else?"

"No, honey, nothing else. We're just going to sit and chat for a bit. Is Bailey working today?" Goldie Johnson asked.

"No, ma'am, she's not working today. She's only here when we're short on help."

"How is she feeling?" Goldie nodded as she spoke.

"She's feeling great and she and Cody're excited about the baby."

"Honey, did that grandson of mine ever write to you?" Elsbeth stirred two creamers into the tiny coffee cup and turned the liquid nearly white.

Lance had taken a job in Georgia shortly after the two of them broke up. And she hadn't really missed him. She realized now that she had been more in love with the idea of love than in love with Lance. It had been wrong to start a relationship based on a desire to be a part of this town, a family and something that would last forever.

"No, Miss Jenkins, I haven't heard from him. Is he doing okay in Atlanta?"

"Oh, I don't know. You know how men are, they don't talk a lot. But I'm really sorry that things didn't work out between the two of you."

The cowbell over the door banged and clanged. Lacey looked up, glad for the distraction. And then not so glad. Jay walked in, blue-and-gray uniform starched and pressed. He looked her way and then looked the other way.

She swallowed and started to move away from the Golden Girls but one of them stopped her. "Honey, now that's a boy that needs a good woman like you."

"No, I don't think so." Lacey smiled anyway.

Jay sat down with a couple of guys close to his age. They were dusty from work and their boots had tracked in half the dirt from the farm. Lacey had just finished sweeping up before the Golden Girls came in.

"Would you like coffee?" She asked because she knew he'd say no. He always did, and it was fun to watch his eyes narrow when she asked.

"Water, and a burger. No fries." He moved the menu to the side.

"Extra lettuce." *Health nut.* She smiled. "Be just a few minutes."

"Thanks." He didn't look at her.

"You roping tonight?" one of the other guys asked Jay as she walked away.

"Yeah, I'm working with a horse that a guy from Tulsa brought up to me."

"How does it feel to be home?" the other guy, Joey, asked.

Lacey paused at the door to the kitchen to hear him say, "It's always good to come home."

When Lacey took Jay his burger, he actually smiled. She refilled his water glass and turned, but a hand caught hers. Not Jay's hand.

"Hey, Lacey, how about you come to the rodeo with me tonight?" Joey Gaston winked and his hand remained on hers.

Lacey pulled her hand free. She could feel heat sliding up her cheeks and she couldn't look at Jay. "I don't think so, Joey."

"Oh, come on, we'd have a good time." He smiled, showing dimples that probably charmed a lot of girls.

"I'm not into a 'good time,' Joey." She wasn't good enough to take home to meet their families, but she was good enough for a back road on a Saturday night.

Lance had done that for her.

"Leave her alone, Joey." Jay's voice, quiet but firm.

Lacey couldn't look at Jay, but she knew that tone in his voice. And Joey knew it, too. He sat back in his chair, staring at Jay, brows raised.

"I was just kidding. I've got a girlfriend."

"Oh, that makes it *way* more amusing, Joey." Lacey walked away, pretending no one stared and that she hadn't been humiliated.

For six years she'd been accepted in Gibson. Dating Lance had been the mistake that changed everything.

She walked through the swinging doors into the kitchen and leaned against the wall. The doors swung open and Jolynn was there. "Honey, don't you listen to those boys. Remember, they're just young pups that need to have their ears boxed. The people who count, the people who love you, know better."

Lacey nodded, and wiped away the tear that broke loose and trickled down her cheek. "I know. Thanks, Jo."

"You can always count on me, sweetie. You know you're my kid and I love you."

The one tear multiplied and Jolynn hugged her tight, the way a mother would hug a daughter. The way Lacey had only dreamed of when she'd been a child growing up.

Chapter Four

Lacey pulled up the driveway to her house and then just sat in the car, too tired to get out. After a long breakfast and lunch shift at the diner, her feet were killing her and her head ached.

She didn't want to deal with Corry after dealing with Joey back at the diner. She didn't want to clean the house after cleaning tables all day. It would have been great to come home and sit by herself on the front porch.

Instead she knew she had to go inside and face her sister. She had to face that dinner probably wasn't cooked, and Corry probably wasn't any more appreciative today than she'd been yesterday.

As she walked up the steps a car drove past. Jay in his truck coming home from work. She waved and he waved back. He was going to the rodeo tonight. She used to go a lot, but not lately. Lately had been about work and classes, and when she had spare time, she studied.

She opened the front door and walked into the slightly muggy house, not completely cool because the window air conditioners were old. A huge mess greeted her.

"What in the world is going on here?" Lacey walked into

her beautiful new living room with the hardwood floors and cobalt-blue braided rugs. From the arched doorway she could see through the dining room to the kitchen with the white-painted cabinets.

Everything was a mess. Clothes littered the floors. Dirty dishes covered the counters and trash covered the floor. A radio blasted rock music and the baby was crying.

"Corry, where are you?" Lacey picked up the wailing baby and hurried through the house.

"I'm here." A voice mumbled from the back porch.

"What are you doing, taking a nap? You have a baby to feed. The house is a disaster and you were supposed to cook."

Corry was curled up on the wicker couch, hair straggling across her face. She was wearing the same clothes she'd worn the previous day. Lacey leaned over, looking into eyes that were blurry and a smile that drooped.

"What have you done?" Lacey reached for the phone, ready to call 911.

"Cold medicine. Just cold medicine."

"How much."

"Just enough. Get off my back."

"Did you have to trash my house?"

Lacey walked away, still holding Rachel close. Words were rolling through her mind, wanting to come out. She couldn't say what she wanted to say. She couldn't stand next to her sister, for fear she would hurt her. Corry was already hurting herself.

"I'm so angry with you, Corry. I can't believe you would do this. You have a baby." Lacey stopped in front of the corner curio in the living room and started picking up the few dogs that had been knocked off the shelves.

"Stop being a prude," Corry snarled.

"Stop being selfish."

"I have a friend coming to get me next week." Corry sat up, leaning forward, her stringy dark hair hanging down over her face.

"How did you call a friend?"

"I used your boyfriend's phone. His mother let me in."

"Leave Mrs. Blackhorse alone." Lacey crossed back to her sister, kneeling in front of her and turning Corry's face so that they made eye contact. "Stay away from Jay and his family."

"Why? Are you afraid of what they'll think of you if they meet me?" Corry smiled a hazy smile. "Too late. I think they were impressed."

Lacey stood back up. The baby cried against her shoulder, reminding her that it was time to eat. "I can't have you living here like this, Corry."

She couldn't let Corry destroy everything she'd built. Lacey had a life here, and friends. She belonged. For the first time in her life, she'd found a place where she belonged.

"I plan on leaving. I'm not going to stay and live like a hermit." Corry's words reminded Lacey of the phone call.

And the crying baby. "You can't take Rachel back to St. Louis. That isn't good for her. How are you going to take care of her if you can't take care of yourself?"

"I'll manage. Don't worry about me. Remember, I'm a woman and we know how to take care of babies. It's easy, right?"

"It isn't easy, Corry. I know that. But this baby deserves a chance. And it's her that I'm worried about, not you."

She walked away because she couldn't argue. And the baby needed to be fed. She could concentrate on Rachel and let the rest go.

She was heating the bottle when Corry walked into the room. Rachel squirmed against Lacey, tiny hands brushing Lacey's face. Corry looked through blurry eyes, but maybe she was also sorry. Lacey wanted her to be sorry.

"Corry, this can't be the life you want for yourself."

"What's wrong with my life?"

"It doesn't include faith. It doesn't include you wanting a better life for yourself and your child."

"I'm here."

"Yes, you are here." Lacey tested the formula on her wrist and cradled Rachel to feed her. Corry only watched.

"Do you like that cowboy?" Corry leaned against the counter. She shoved her trembling hands into her pockets and hunkered down, defeated.

Lacey ignored the obvious signs of someone going through withdrawal. She knew that was the reason for the cold medicine. Her sister would have done anything for a high at this point.

"He isn't even a friend, just someone I know from town and from church."

For a minute it felt like a normal conversation between sisters. To keep up the illusion, Lacey kept her gaze averted.

"I think I could have more luck with him. You're too pushy." The normal moment between sisters ended with that comment.

Lacey lifted Rachel to her shoulder and patted the baby's back. "Stop it, Corry."

"Are you jealous?"

"There's nothing to be jealous of. I don't want him used. End of story."

"When did you get all righteous? Does he know what you used to be?"

Lacey turned to face her sister. She could feel heat crawling up her neck to her cheeks. "My past is behind me. And it wasn't who I…" She blinked a few times, wishing there weren't tears in her eyes. "It wasn't who I wanted to be."

She didn't belong. Not the way she really wanted to belong to Gibson. After all of these years, she wasn't really one of them. She wanted to be like these people, growing up here, having lifelong friends, family that never moved away, and a place that was all hers.

"Not so easy to be a goody-goody now, is it? Not with me here to remind you of what you used to be. What you still are."

Take a deep breath, she told herself. She wasn't that girl from St. Louis, not here in Gibson. Her past was forgiven. She had to remember who she was now, and who she was in Christ. *For God so loved the world that He gave His only begotten son.*

She was the "whosoever" who had chosen to believe in Jesus. She would not perish, but have everlasting life. They sang a song in church, "My Sins Are Gone." It was her song. Anyone could ask her why she was happy, how she could smile and go on, building a new life. The answer was simple: because her sins were gone, as far as east from west. Her sister could remind her, but she couldn't bring back what had been forgiven. Not really.

"I'm a Christian, Corry. I have faith. I have a new life, and that old life is no longer a part of me."

"Really? You might want to think it's gone, but it's still there."

"I am who I am because of my past, Corry. But God gave me a new life."

"And what makes you so special?"

"I'm not special. I made a choice that anyone can make."

"A past isn't that easy to get rid of." Corry shook her head and walked off, tossing the words over her shoulder. "You're the one living in a fantasy world. By the way, someone's here."

Jay knocked on the door because he had promised Cody and Bailey he would. They'd been trying to call Lacey, but she wasn't answering her cell phone. They were worried. He could have told them that Lacey Gould could take care of herself, but they wouldn't have listened.

They were a lot like his mom, determined to make sure Lacey was kept safe. As if she needed protection.

From the sounds coming from inside the house, he guessed that right now she wanted rid of her sister. He knocked again.

She opened the door, hair a little shaggier than normal and liner under her eyes a little smudged. She didn't smile.

"Bailey wanted me to stop and check on you."

"Why?"

"She's been trying to call and she can't get hold of you."

Lacey reached into her pocket and pulled out her cell phone. She frowned at it and then slipped it back into her pocket. "No signal."

"Okay, I'll let them know." He glanced past her. "What happened?"

"Nothing." Her eyes narrowed, and she shook her head a little, as if she really didn't understand his question.

"Lacey, is everything okay?"

"Fine." She glanced over her shoulder, at the mess, at the broken dogs, at the clothes scattered on the floor. "I'm sorry, I'll get it cleaned up."

"I'm not talking about the house. I know you'll get it cleaned up. I'm asking if *you're* okay."

The baby was crying, and the radio played from the kitchen. Lacey Gould's eyes watered and her nose turned pink.

"Let me help you clean up." He walked past her, into the ransacked house. "Is she looking for a fix?"

"She is." Lacey walked away from him. "Let me get the baby."

"I'll get a broom."

"You don't have to. You have somewhere you need to be and I'm here for the night. It won't take me long to clean up." She walked back into the room with the baby cuddled against her. Exhaustion etched lines across her face and her shoulders heaved with a sigh.

Jay offered her a smile that he knew wouldn't ease her worry or take away the burden. Instead he bent and started picking up the dog figurines that were still intact. The dogs meant something to her. He thought it was more about a life she had never had than a pet she wanted.

"We could get her help." He offered the suggestion as he put the last dog in place. "We could try for a seventy-two hour hold and maybe get her into a treatment program."

"She has to want help."

"I guess you're right." He stood up straight. He hadn't realized before that she was a good half-foot shorter than his six feet two inches.

He felt as though he towered over her.

"Thanks for stopping by, Jay. If you see Bailey, tell her I'm fine."

"You could ride along and tell her yourself. It probably would be good for you to get out for a while."

"Ride along?" She stared and then shook her head. "I don't think you want to start that rumor."

"It won't start rumors."

"It would, and you really don't want your name linked to mine."

He didn't. She was right. He didn't want his name linked to anyone else's name because three years of Cindy had cured him of his dreams of getting married, having the picket fence and a few kids. He didn't want a woman that would only be a replacement for what he'd lost years ago. Somewhere along the way Cindy had figured that out.

The baby was crying. "I can't go, Jay. Corry is strung out and I can't leave the baby here."

"Bring the baby."

Her eyes widened. For a long moment she stood there, staring at him, staring at the door. Finally she nodded.

"I will go." She hurried into the kitchen and came back with a diaper bag and the baby still held against her shoulder. "But I have to change clothes first. I smell like a cheeseburger."

"Okay." He didn't expect her to shove the baby into his arms, but she did. The wiggling infant fit into the crook of his elbow, her hands grasping at the air. "Umm, Lacey, the baby..."

She had already reached the bedroom door. "What?"

How did he admit to this? Honesty seemed to be the answer, but he knew he wouldn't get sympathy. "I've never held a baby."

"You've never held a baby. Isn't your dad an OB-GYN? And you've never held a baby?"

"Never." He swallowed a little because his heart was doing a funny dance as he held this baby and he couldn't stop looking at Lacey Gould. And she had the nerve to laugh at him.

"Sit down before you drop her. You look a little pale."

He sat down, still clutching the tiny little girl in his arms. He smiled down at her, and man if she didn't smile back, her grin half-tilted and making her nose scrunch.

"Now aren't you something else." He leaned, talking softly, and she smiled again. "You're a little charmer. I think I'd just about buy you a pony."

"She wants a bay." Lacey was back, still smiling. She had changed into jeans and a peasant top that flowed out over the top of her jeans. Her hair spiked around her face and she had wiped away the smudged liner.

"Ready to go?" He handed the baby over, still unsure with her in his arms. And as he looked at Lacey Gould, she was one more thing that he was suddenly unsure about.

"I'm ready to go."

He held the door and let Lacey walk out first, because he was afraid to walk out next to her, afraid of what it might feel like to be close to her when she smelled like lavender.

* * *

Lacey leaned close to the window, trying not to look like an overanxious puppy leaning out the truck as they drove onto the rodeo grounds. Stock trailers were parked along the back section and cars were parked in the field next to the arena.

She had been before, more times than she could count, but never like this, in a truck with a stock trailer hooked to the back and a cowboy sitting in the seat next to her. Riding with Bailey and Cody didn't count, not this way. If other girls dreamed of fairy-tale dances and diamonds, Lacey dreamed of this, of boots and cowboys and horses.

Not so much the cowboys these days, but still…

"Don't fall out." Jay smiled as he said it, white teeth flashing in a suntanned face. His hat was on the seat next to him and his dark hair that brushed his collar showed the ring where the hat had been.

She shifted in the seat and leaned back. "I guess you're not at all excited?"

"Of course I am. I've been living in the city for eight years. Longer if you count college. It's good to be home full-time."

"What events are you in?"

"A little of everything. I mainly team rope. But every now and then I ride a bull."

"I want to ride a bull." She hadn't meant to sound like a silly girl, but his eyes widened and he shook his head.

"Maybe you could try barrel racing?" He made the suggestion without looking at her.

"Okay."

Anything. It was all a part of the dream package she'd created for herself. She wanted this life, with these people. For a long time she'd wanted love and acceptance.

She'd found those things in Gibson. Now she wanted horses

and a farm of her own. Jay wouldn't understand that dream; he'd always had those things.

"Lacey, we're not that different. This has been my life, but I came home to reclaim what I left behind."

"And it cost you?"

"It cost me." He slowed, and then eased back into a space next to another truck and trailer.

"Are you team roping tonight?" She looked back, at the pricked ears of the horse in the trailer.

"Yeah, and I think I have to ride a bull. Cody signed me up. He says he needs a little competition from time to time."

"Because Bailey is keeping him close to home." She bit down on her bottom lip and looked out the window.

The truck stopped, the trailer squeaking behind it, coming to a halt. The horse whinnied and other horses answered. From the pens behind the arena, cattle mooed, restless from being corralled for so long.

Lacey breathed deep, loving it all. And the man next to her…she glanced in his direction. He was a surprise. He had invited her.

And she had to process that information.

Time to come back to earth, and to remember what it felt like to be hurt, to have her trust stomped on. Lacey unbuckled the baby and pulled her out of the seat, a good distraction because Rachel's eyes were open and she smiled that baby half-smile. Drool trickled down her baby chin.

"Do you think Corry will stay?" Jay had unbuckled his seat belt and he pulled the keys from the ignition of the truck.

The question was one that Lacey had considered, but didn't want to. It made her heart ache to think of Corry leaving, not knowing where she would take the baby. Lacey shrugged and pulled Rachel, cooing and soft, close to her.

"I really don't know. I don't want to think about that." She kissed the baby's cheek. "But I guess I should."

"Maybe she'll stay."

"She won't. She's restless. She's always been restless."

"I understand restless." He stepped out of the truck.

Lacey, baby in her arms and diaper bag over her shoulder, followed. She met up with him at the back of the trailer. The small glimpse into his life intrigued her. He'd never been open.

"You don't seem restless." She stood back as he opened the trailer and led the horse out. Not his horse, he'd explained, but one he was training. The animal was huge, with a golden-brown coat that glistened.

He glanced at her, shrugging and then went back to the horse. He pulled a saddle out of the tack compartment of the trailer. Expertly tooled and polished, the leather practically glowed in the early evening light.

The lights of the arena came on and Lacey knew that the bleachers would be filling up. But she couldn't walk away because Jay had stories, just like everyone else.

"How could you be restless?" She pushed, forgetting for a moment that he was little more than a stranger.

"Why is that so unusual?" He had the saddle on the horse and was pulling the girth strap tight around the animal's middle. The horse, a gentle giant, stood still, head low and ears pricked forward.

"You don't seem restless."

"Really? And what makes you think you know anything about me?" He straightened, tall and all cowboy in new Wranglers and worn boots. His western shirt was from the mall, not the farm store.

Contradictions. And she loved a mystery.

"So, tell me." She waited, holding the baby in the crook of her arm, but dropping the diaper bag.

"I grew up on a farm in a small town, Lacey. I wanted to live in the city, to experience life in an apartment with close neighbors."

"And you loved it?" She smiled, because he couldn't have.

He grinned back at her. "I did, for a while. But then the new wore off and it was just noise, traffic and the smell of exhaust."

"So you came home because you got tired of city life?"

"I came home." And he didn't finish, but she knew that he'd come home because of a broken heart. Sometimes she saw it in his eyes. Sometimes he looked like someone who had been broken, but was gluing the pieces back together.

"Your parents are glad."

"I know they are." He slipped the reins over the neck of the horse. "And Lacey, before you start thinking I'm one of those poor strays behind the diner, I'm not. Cindy didn't break my heart."

He winked. For a moment she almost believed that his heart hadn't been broken. For a fleeting second she wanted to hold him. To be held by a cowboy with strong arms and roots that went deep in a community.

"I didn't…" She didn't know what to say. She didn't need to know? Or she didn't plan on trying to fix him?

"You did. Your eyes get all weepy and you look like you've found someone who needs fixing. I don't. I'm glad to be home."

He was standing close to her, and she hadn't realized before that his presence would suck the air out of her space, not until that moment. Her lungs tightened inside her chest and she took a step back, kissing the baby's head to distract her thoughts from the man, all cowboy, standing in front of her.

He cocked his head to the side and his mouth opened, but then closed and he shook his head. "I need to find Cody."

"Of course." She backed away. "I'll meet up with you later."

And later she would have her thoughts back in control and she wouldn't be thinking of him as the cowboy who picked up those silly dog figurines and put them back on the shelf while she swept up the pieces of what had been broken.

Chapter Five

Lacey hurried away, ignoring the desire to glance over her shoulder, to see if he was watching. He wouldn't watch. He would get on his horse, shaking his head because she had climbed into his life that way.

She had no business messing in his life; she was a dirty sock, mistakenly tossed in the basket with the clean socks. She couldn't hide from reality.

Jay was the round peg in the round hole. He fit. He was a part of Gibson and someday, he'd marry a girl from Gibson. And Lacey didn't know why that suddenly bothered her, or why it bothered her that when he looked at her, it was with that look, the one that said she was the community stray, taken in and fed, given a safe place to stay.

The way she fed stray cats behind the diner.

"Hey, Lacey, up here."

She looked up, searching the crowd. When she saw Bailey, she waved. Bailey had a seat midway up the bleachers, with a clear view of the chutes. Lacey climbed the steps and squeezed past a couple of people to take a seat next to her friend.

"I didn't expect to see you here." Bailey held her hands out and took the baby, her own belly growing rounder every day.

"Long story." Lacey searched the crowd of men behind the pens. She sought a tall cowboy wearing a white hat, his shirt plaid. She found him, standing next to the buckskin and talking to one of the other guys.

"Make it a short story and fill me in." Bailey leaned a shoulder against Lacey's. "You okay?"

"Hmmm?" Lacey nodded. She didn't want to talk, not here, with hundreds of people surrounding them, eating popcorn or cotton candy and drinking soda from paper cups.

"Are you okay?" Louder voice now, a little impatient.

"I'm great." Lacey leaned back on the bleacher seat. "My sister wrecked my house and she's passed out in my bed. The cowboy that lives down the lane treats me like an interloper. I'm living in his grandparents' house, and he doesn't want me there."

"He brought you tonight."

"He did. I'm a charity case. He felt bad because Corry broke my dogs."

Bailey nodded. "He's about to ride a bull. But since you've sworn off men, I guess that doesn't matter to you?"

"I have a reason for swearing off men. I'm never going to be the type of woman a man takes home to meet his family."

"Lance has problems, Lacey. That isn't about you, it's about him."

"It is about me. It takes a lot for anyone to understand where I've been and what I've done. I'm ashamed of the life I lived, so why should I expect a man to blindly accept my past?"

"You're forgetting what God has done in your life. You're forgetting what He can still do. You're not a finished product. None of us are. Our stories are still being written."

"No, I'm not forgetting." Lacey looked away, because she couldn't admit that sometimes she wondered how God could forgive. How could He take someone as dirty as she felt and turn them into someone people respected?

She worked really hard trying to be that person that others respected.

The bulls ran through the chutes. Lacey leaned back, watching as cowboy after cowboy got tossed. Each time one of them hit the dirt, she cringed. She didn't really want to ride a bull.

"Jay's up." Bailey pointed. Taller than the other bull riders, he stood on the outside of the chute. The bull moved in the chute, a truck-sized animal, pawing the ground.

"I really don't want to watch."

"It isn't easy." Bailey shifted Rachel, now sleeping, on her shoulder. "It doesn't get easier. Every time I watch Cody ride, I pray, close my eyes, peek, pray some more."

"Yes, but you love Cody."

"True. The cowboy in question is just your neighbor."

"Exactly." Lacey laughed and glanced at Bailey, willing to give her friend what she wanted to hear. "He's cute, Bailey, I'm not denying that. But I'm not looking for cute."

"Of course not."

"I'm not looking—period."

"But it is okay to look." Bailey smiled a happy smile and elbowed Lacey. "There he goes."

The gate opened and the bull spun out of the opening, coming up off the ground like a ballet dancer. Amazing that an animal so huge could move like that. The thud when the beast came down jarred the man on his back and Jay fell back, moving his free arm forward.

The buzzer sounded and Jay jumped, landing clear of the animal, but hitting the ground hard. The bull didn't want to let it go. The animal turned on Jay, charging the cowboy, who was slow getting up.

A bullfighter jumped between the beast and the man, giving

Jay just enough time to escape, to jump on the fence and wait for the distracted animal to make up his mind that he'd rather not take a piece out of a cowboy.

Jay looked up, his hat gone. His dark gaze met Lacey's and stayed there, connected, for just a few seconds. Warm brown eyes in a face that was lean and handsome. And then he hopped down from the fence and limped away.

"Breathe," Bailey whispered.

Lacey breathed. It wasn't easy. She inhaled a gulp of air and her heart raced.

The rodeo ended with steer wrestling. Jay watched from behind the pens at the back of the arena, still smarting from the bull, and still thinking about Lacey Gould's dark brown eyes. He shook his head and walked away, back to his trailer and his horse.

"That was quite a ride." Cody slapped Jay on the back as he untied his horse.

"Thanks. I'm glad it made you happy."

"Oh, come on, you enjoyed it." Cody leaned against the side of the trailer, his hat pushed back on his head. "You'll do it again next week."

"I'm thinking no." Jay tightened his grip on Buck's reins because the horse was tossing his head, whinnying to a nearby mare. "I think I'll stick to roping."

"Yeah, I think I'm done with bull riding, too. I've got a baby on the way."

"Right, that does sound like a good reason to stop."

"Yeah, it does." Cody smiled like a guy who had it all. And he did. He had the wife, a child, the farm and a baby on the way. Jay had a diamond ring in a drawer and a room in his parents' house. He had a box of memories that he kept hidden in a closet.

"Speaking of wives and babies, I'm going to find my wife." Cody slapped him on the back again and walked away.

Jay pulled the saddle off the horse and limped to the back of his truck, his knee stiff and his back even stiffer. He tossed the saddle in the back of the truck and then leaned for a minute, wishing again that he hadn't ridden that bull. Bull riding wasn't a sport a guy jumped into.

He tried not to think about Lacey's face in the crowd, pale and wide-eyed as she watched him scramble to the fence, escaping big hooves and an animal that wanted to hurt him.

The horse whinnied, reminding him of work that still needed to be done. He walked back to the animal, rubbing Buck's sleek neck and then pulling off the bridle, leaving just the halter and lead rope. The horse nodded his head as if he approved.

"I'm getting too old for crazy stunts, Buck."

"You stayed on." The feminine voice from behind him was a little soft, a little teasing.

"Yep."

He turned and smiled at Lacey. She wasn't a friend, just someone his mom had picked up and brought home. He had friends, people he'd grown up with, gone to church with, known all his life. He didn't know where to put her, because she didn't fit those categories. Someone that he knew? A person that needed help? Someone passing through?

He would have preferred she stayed in Jolynn's apartment, not the house his grandparents had built. Jamie's house. But she was there now, and he'd deal with it. He moved away from his horse and straightened, raising his hands over his head to stretch the kinks out of his back.

She was here tonight, in his life, because he'd brought her. He had been trying not to think about that, or why he'd extended the offer. Maybe because of the pain in her eyes when she'd looked at those silly dogs her sister had broken.

Who got upset over something like that?

Lacey took cautious steps forward. She held the sleeping

baby in one arm and had the diaper bag over her shoulder. She didn't carry a purse.

"You actually did pretty well," she encouraged, a shy smile on a face that shouldn't have been shy. He had never seen her as shy. She was the waitress who never backed down when the guys at the diner gave her a hard time.

"I did stay on, but it wasn't fun and it isn't something I want to do again. I think I'll stick to roping."

"You won the roping event." She moved forward, her hand sliding up the rump of his horse. "Want me to do something?"

"No, I've got it."

She stood next to him, her hand on his horse's neck. She didn't look at him, and he wondered why. Did she think that by not looking at him, she could hide her secrets?

"I'm going to put the baby in the truck." She moved away and he let her go. Buck pushed at him with his big, tan head, rubbing his jaw against Jay's shoulder.

"In the trailer, Buck." Jay opened the trailer and moved to the side. Buck went in, his hooves pounding on the floor of the trailer, rattling the metal sides as his weight shifted and settled.

"He's an amazing animal." Lacey had returned, without the baby. He was tying the horse to the front of the trailer. "When you rope on him, it's like he knows what you want him to do before you make a move."

"He's a smart animal." Jay latched the trailer.

"Thank you for letting me come with you tonight."

Jay shrugged, another movement that didn't feel too great. He stepped back against his trailer and brought her with him, because the truck next to them was pulling forward.

"I didn't mind." His hand was still on her arm.

She looked from his hand on her arm to his face. Her teeth bit into her bottom lip and she shivered, maybe from the cold night air.

It was dark and the band was playing. Jay could see people two-stepping on a temporary dance floor. Couples scooted in time to the music, and children ran in the open field, catching fireflies.

Lacey smelled like lavender and her arm was soft. She looked up, her eyes dark in a face that was soft, but tough. He moved his hand from her arm and touched her cheek.

She shook her head a little and took a step back, disengaging from his touch. But that small step didn't undo the moment. She was street-smart and vulnerable and he wanted to see how she felt in his arms.

He wanted to brush away the hurt look in her eyes, and the shame that caused her to look away too often. Instead, he came to his senses and pulled back, letting the moment slip away.

"We should go." Lacey stepped over the tongue of the trailer and put distance between them. Her arms were crossed and she had lost the vulnerable look. "Jay, whatever that was, it wasn't real."

"What?"

"It was moonlight. It was summertime and soft music. It was you being lonely and losing someone you thought you'd spend your life with."

"Maybe you're right."

"I am right. But I'm nobody's moment. Someday I want forever, but I'll never be a moment again."

He exhaled a deep breath and whistled low. "Okay, then I guess we should go."

He felt like the world's biggest loser.

Lacey woke up on Sunday morning, glad that she had a day off. If only she'd gotten some sleep, but she hadn't. Jay had dropped her off at midnight, and wound up from the night, she'd stayed up for two hours, cleaning.

She rolled over in bed, listening to the sound of country life drifting through the open window. Cows mooed from the field and somewhere a rooster crowed. He was a little late, but still trying to tell everyone that it was time to get up.

The baby cried and she heard Corry telling her to shush, as if the baby would listen and not expect to be fed. Lacey sat up and stretched. She had an hour to get ready before church.

When she walked through the door of the dining room, Corry was at the table with a bowl of cereal. Rachel was in the bassinet, arms flailing the air.

"Have you fed her?" Lacey picked up the tiny infant and held her close. The baby fussed too much. "Has she been to a doctor?"

"Give me a break. Like I have the money for that. She's fine."

"She's hungry and she feels warm."

"So, feed her, mother of the year."

"I'm not her mother, Corry."

Corry drank the milk from her bowl and took it to the sink. At least she did that much. Lacey took a deep breath and exhaled the brewing impatience. The baby curled against her shoulder, fist working in her tiny mouth.

"I'll feed her, you get ready for church." Lacey held the baby with one arm and reached in the drainer at the edge of the sink for a clean bottle.

"I'm not going to church."

"If you're staying with me, you're going to church."

"Make me go and you'll regret it."

"I probably will, but you're going." Lacey shook the bottle to mix the formula with the water. "I've already taken a shower. You can have yours now."

She turned away from Corry, but shuddered when the bathroom door slammed. "Well, little baby, this is probably something I'll pay for."

Rachel sucked at the bottle, draining it in no time and then burping loudly against Lacey's shoulder. She put the sleeping baby into the infant car seat and was strapping her in as Corry walked out of the bathroom. She wore a black miniskirt and a white tank top.

"You can't wear that."

"It's all I have." Gum smacked and Corry busied herself, far too happily, shoving diapers and wipes along with an extra bottle into the bag.

Rachel cried, a little restless and fussy.

"I think she's sick." Corry looked at the baby and then at Lacey. "What do you think?"

"She feels warm and her cheeks are a little pink. I don't know."

Corry unbuckled the straps and pulled Rachel out of the seat. "I think she has a fever."

"Do you have medicine for her?"

Corry nodded. "I have those drops. I'll give her some of those."

"And stay home with her. She shouldn't be out. You can stay here and let her sleep."

Corry's eyes widened. "Really? You're not going to make me go to church."

"I'm not going to make you." Lacey sighed. "Corry, no one can *make* you go to church. I only want you to try to get your life together and stay clean."

"And church is going to make it all better?"

"Church doesn't, but God does. He really does make things better when you trust Him." The act of going to church hadn't changed anything for Lacey. She had tried that routine as a teenager, because she'd known, really known that God could help, but each time she went into a church, thinking it would be a magic cure, it hadn't changed anything. Because she had thought it was about going to church.

In Gibson she had learned that it was about faith, about trusting God, not about going to church wishing people would love her. She had learned, too, about loving herself.

She needed to remember that, she realized. Since Lance, she'd had a tough time remembering her own clean slate and that she was worth loving.

Corry pushed through the diapers and wipes in the diaper bag and pulled out infant drops. She held them out to Lacey. "How much do I give her?"

Lacey took the bottle and looked at the back, reading the directions. "One dropper. And don't give her more until I get home. I'll be late, though. You'll have to fix your own lunch."

"Where are you going?"

"After church there are a few of us that go to the nursing home to sing and have church with the people there."

"Ah, isn't that sweet."

Lacey let it go. "I'll see you later."

Today Jay would be joining them at the nursing home. She wondered how the return of one man to his hometown could change everything. For years Gibson had been her safe place. Jay's presence undid that feeling.

Chapter Six

Jay looked across the room and caught the gaze of Lacey Gould. She sat next to an older woman with snow-white hair and hands that shook. They were flipping through the pages of a hymnal and talking in low tones that didn't carry.

But from time to time Lacey looked up at him. This time he caught her staring, and he hadn't expected the look in her eyes to be wariness. She didn't trust him.

Distracted, he dropped his guitar pick. He leaned to pick it up and Bailey kicked his shin. He nearly said something, but the way she was smiling, he couldn't. She'd been teasing him for twenty-some years. She probably wasn't going to stop now.

For years she'd been the little girl on the bus that he looked out for, and sometimes wanted to escape. She'd sent him a love note once. She'd been thirteen, he was sixteen. When he told her it wouldn't work, she cried and told her dad on him.

"She's a good person, Jay," Bailey whispered.

"I'm sure she is." He remembered that Bailey also had a good left hook and he didn't want to make her mad.

He didn't doubt that Lacey was a good person. He had watched her at church, making the rounds and speaking to everyone before the service began. As soon as church ended, she said her good-byes and drove to the nursing home.

He had questions about her community service, but it wasn't any of his business. It should be up to Pastor Dan, or even Bailey, to explain to Lacey Gould that God wasn't expecting her to earn forgiveness through good works.

"What song do we sing first?" Lacey asked from across the room. The sweet-faced older lady had her arm through Lacey's.

Jay lifted his guitar and shrugged. He grimaced at the jab of pain in his lower back and Lacey grinned, because she knew that a bull had dumped him hard the night before.

"'In the Garden'?" He didn't need music for that one.

Lacey knew it; she was nodding and turning the pages of the hymnal. Her elderly friend clapped and smiled, saying it was one of her favorites, and then her eyes grew misty.

"My husband is there waiting for me in that garden." She said it in such a soft and wavering voice that Jay barely heard. He did see tears shimmering in Lacey's eyes, from compassion, always compassion. He wondered if she felt the emotions of everyone she met.

Lacey held the woman's hand and as Jay started to play, Lacey led the song, her voice alto and clear, the meaning of the words clearly written on her face. The wavering voice of her friend joined in, sweet and soprano.

Jay stumbled over the chords and caught up. Next to him, Bailey giggled, the way she'd done on the bus years ago. He was glad she was still getting enjoyment out of his life. He'd been gone nearly eight years, working on the Springfield PD, and it felt as if he'd never left.

Over the next thirty minutes, he found firm footing again. He forgot Lacey and concentrated on the music as the people gathered in the circle around them. He had missed Gibson. He had missed these people, some of whom he had known all of his life. The gentleman to his left had been his high school principal. One of the ladies had lived down the road from his family.

Most of the kids from Gibson had moved to the city or left the state. So many of the people in the nursing home were without close family these days, and this touch from their church made the difference.

Lacey made the difference, he realized. With her flashy smile and soft laughter, her teasing comments and warm hugs, she made a difference that he hadn't expected.

In the lives of these people.

"Not interested, huh?" Bailey teased as they finished up and he was putting his guitar away.

"Interested in what? Helping with this ministry? Of course I am."

"In Lacey."

"Go away, Bailey. You're starting to be a fifth-grade pest."

"Write her a note and ask her out."

"You stink at matchmaking. Matchmakers are supposed to be sneaky, a little underhanded."

Bailey laughed, her eyes watering. "Oh, thank you, now that I know the finer points of the art, I'll do better next time. Maybe you should learn the fine art of realizing when a woman is perfect for you."

"That's obviously a lesson I never learned." He closed the case on his guitar. He saw Lacey walk out as if she had somewhere to be. "Bailey, I'm not interested. I really thought I'd found the right woman, and I dated her for three years only to find out she wasn't interested in a cowboy. So if you don't mind, I'm on vacation from romance and I'm boycotting matchmakers."

Bailey's laughter faded, so did her smile. "She didn't hurt you, Jay. You're still thinking about Jamie. Maybe it's time to let her go?"

Gut-stomped in the worst way, by a woman with a soft

smile. He smiled down at Bailey, happy for her, and sorry that she knew all of his secrets.

"I'm trying, Bay. I really am. I guess that's why I decided to come home. Because I have to face it here, and I have to deal with it."

"I'm sorry, Jay. I thought that enough time had gone by and I was hoping you were ready to move on."

"You were wrong." He smiled to soften the words, because Bailey had been a friend his entire life. A pest, but a friend.

"So, you've given up on love?"

"For now. I want to build my house and get settled back into my life here. I'll be thirty this winter and maybe I'm just going to be a settled old bachelor, raising my horses and doing a little singing for church."

"What a nice dream." She patted his arm, not the slap on the back that Cody had given him the night before. She was getting all maternal. "See you later."

He nodded and picked up his guitar. When he walked out the front entrance of the nursing home, it was hot, unbearably hot. He pulled sunglasses out of his pocket and slid them on as he walked across the parking lot. The sound of an engine cranking, not firing, caught his attention.

Of course it would be Lacey. They were the only ones left and she was sitting in her car with the driver's side door open.

Jay put his guitar in the front of his truck and walked over to her car. "Won't start?"

"Nope." She tried again. "It always starts. Why won't it start now?"

He shrugged. Probably Bailey did something to it, something less conspicuous than just telling him he should ask Lacey out. He smiled at the thought, because he could picture Bailey out here removing the coil wire from Lacey's car. But she wouldn't do that. He didn't think she would.

"Pop the hood and I'll take a look."

She did and he walked to the front of the car to push the hood up. The coil wire was there. He smiled. Nothing looked out of place.

"Lacey, it isn't out of gas, is it?" He peeked around the raised hood at her.

"I don't think so." And then she groaned. "First the mower and now this."

"I'll drive you home and we'll come back later with gas."

"I can't believe I did that." She got out of the car and closed the door. "I always make sure it has gas."

"Not today."

She shook her head. "I'm not sure what's wrong with me."

"You have a lot going on in your life." He opened the passenger-side door of his truck. "Maybe having today off will help."

"Maybe."

Jay closed the door and walked around to the driver's side with a quick look up, wondering what God was thinking. He got in and started his truck. Lacey kept her face turned, staring out the passenger-side window.

He wondered if she was crying.

The front door of the house was open. Lacey sat in Jay's truck, her stomach tightening, because it didn't look right. She glanced at Jay, who had remained silent during the drive home. She hadn't had much to say, either.

What did you say to a stranger whose life you felt like you were invading?

"Do you always leave the front door of the house open?" He turned off the truck.

"Of course I don't. Something's wrong." She reached for the door handle and started to get out of the truck.

Jay's hand on her arm stopped her. "No, let me go in first."

"Don't say that." Her skin prickled with cold heat. "Don't say it like something has happened."

"Nothing has happened, but we're not taking chances."

She nodded, swallowing past the lump that lodged between her heart and her throat. Jay got out of the truck and walked up to the house. He eased up to the front door and looked inside. Then he stepped through the opening into the dark house.

Lacey waited, her heart pounding, thudding in her chest. She should have known that something like this would happen. Whatever *this* was. She didn't even know, but she knew without a doubt that something was wrong.

Jay walked back onto the porch and shook his head. He motioned her out of the truck. Lacey grabbed her Bible and got out. She walked to the front porch, not wanting to hear what she knew he would tell her.

"There's no one in here."

"Maybe she went for a walk. Or she might have gone to use your phone." Grasping, she knew she was grasping at straws.

And Jay was just being the nice guy that he was by staying, by not making accusations.

"That's possible," he finally said.

"She might have left a note, telling me where she went."

"Okay. We can look." But he didn't believe it. Lacey didn't know why that hurt, but it did. Because it felt like he didn't believe her, or trust her. She was an extension of Corry, because they had come from the same place.

She walked into the house and he followed, slower, taking more time. "I knew I should have made her go to church."

"You can't force someone."

"I know, but if I had, she'd be here and Rachel would be safe."

Lacey wouldn't feel so frantic, like some unseen clock was ticking, telling her she was nearly out of time. And she didn't know why, or what would happen when the time ran out.

"Lacey." He stood in front of the desk where she kept her bills and other paperwork. "You know she has a record, right?"

Lacey turned, and he was watching her, pretending it was a normal question. "I do know."

She wanted to ask him if he knew that *she* had a record. Did he know what she had done to put food on the table, to pay the rent to keep the roof over her younger siblings' heads? She looked away, because she didn't really want answers to those questions from him.

It was too much information, and it would let him too far into her life, and leave her open to whatever look might be in his eyes.

It might be too much like the look in Lance's eyes when he'd said he could love her no matter what. With Jay it was different; they hadn't stepped into each other's lives that way. He just happened to be here with her now.

"Lacey, do you know who she's been in contact with?"

"No." She stood in the doorway of Corry's room. The bedding was flung across the bed and dragged on the floor, and a few odds and ends of clothing were still scattered about.

Jay walked into the room, an envelope in his hand.

"She's gone. This was on the table." He handed her an envelope.

Lacey's fingers trembled as she took it from him. She ripped it and tore the paper out. Eyes watering, she read the scribbled lines, trying to make sense of misspelled words and her sister's childlike handwriting. But she got it. She crumpled the note in her hand. She got it.

"She's gone." She held out the note and Jay took it from her hand.

"Let's take a drive and see if we can find her. She couldn't have gotten far."

Optimism. Lacey had worked hard on being an optimist. She

had worked hard on finding faith in hard times. She didn't know what to think about Corry leaving with the baby.

She glanced at her watch. "Jay, if they left right after I left, they could be back in St. Louis by now."

He inhaled and let it out in a sigh. "That's true. Let's go inside and we'll see if she left anything behind."

"We should call the police."

Dark brows lifted and he sort of smiled at her. "Lacey, I am the police. And unless she's committed a crime, there's no reason for going after her. She's a grown woman who left your house with her own child."

"But she can't take care of Rachel. She can barely take care of herself."

"She's an adult."

"An adult who reads and writes at a first-grade level." Lacey looked away from his compassion, his sympathy.

"Can she take care of Rachel?"

Lacey walked through the dark, cool interior of the house, her house. She kept her eyes down, thinking of what to do next. She couldn't face the empty bassinet or thoughts of Rachel with Corry.

"She can, but I don't know if she can keep her safe." Lacey spoke softly, because if she said it too loudly, would it seem harsh? "My mother and Corry make a lot of bad decisions."

"We could hotline her with family services and maybe they could intervene on behalf of the baby." Jay walked through the kitchen. He stopped at the canisters.

"What do you keep in these?"

"Sugar, flour, coffee. Normal stuff. Why?"

"This one is empty and the lid was next to it." He lifted the smallest canister.

The air left her lungs and the room felt too hot, and then too cold. Never in a million years would she have thought…

But then again, she should have. Because she knew Corry,

knew what she was capable of. She was capable of stealing from her own family.

"It wasn't coffee?" He set the canister down and replaced the lid. "Money?"

Her chest ached and her throat tightened. "I can't believe I was so stupid."

She wouldn't cry. She wouldn't be the person he pitied. She had survived worse than this, and she would survive again.

"You aren't stupid."

"I should have put it in the bank." She shook her head, looking away from Jay so she wouldn't see his compassion and he couldn't see her tears. "I put my tip money in there, and lived on my hourly wages. It was for land."

"For land?" Soft and tender, his voice soothed. He took a few steps in her direction, and she wanted to rely on the strong arms of a cowboy to hold her and tell her everything would be okay.

He wasn't offering, and she knew better.

"Yes, for land. I want a place of my own." Dreams, snatched away. "But I can start over, right? It isn't the end of the world."

"No." He stood in front of her now, tall and cowboy, with eyes that seemed to understand. "It isn't the end of the world, but it probably feels like it is."

"It feels more like I might never see my niece again. Rachel is more important than land. I don't want that baby to live the life we lived in St. Louis. I want her to have a real family and real chances."

"She'll be okay with her mother."

"No, she won't. Jay, you don't get it. You've lived here all your life, in a cocoon that sheltered you from the outside world. You don't know what it's like to always worry about who's walking through the front door and what they're going to do to you."

The words spilled out and so did the tears, coursing down

her cheeks, salty on her lips. She brushed them away with her hand and shook her head when he tried to hold her.

"Don't look at me like that," she whispered, staring at the floor because she couldn't look him in the eyes. "I don't want to be someone you feel sorry for. I'd much rather you resent me for being here."

"I don't resent you."

She smiled then and wiped at her eyes. "You do, but it's nice of you to say you don't. Look, I'm fine. I survived and I have a great life here. And if you keep looking at me like that, you're going to make me cry again. I don't want to cry anymore."

"We'll find Rachel." He made it sound like a promise she could believe. She'd been promised a lot in her life.

"I hope so."

"Lacey, growing up in Gibson doesn't guarantee anything." He walked to the door. "Let's see if we can find your sister and the baby. At least now we have a reason to call the police."

The stolen money. Lacey picked up her purse and followed him out the door, still hurting over what Corry had done, and ashamed because she knew that life held no guarantees for anyone.

Not even for Jay Blackhorse.

Chapter Seven

Jay cruised past the church on Tuesday afternoon. He'd been past a couple of other times, and each time, Lacey's car had been parked out front. It was still parked out front. Maybe she'd heard from her sister.

Probably not. He didn't expect Corry to suddenly have a conscience and feel guilty for what she'd done to Lacey. He pulled into the church parking lot and parked. But he didn't get out.

Instead, he questioned why he was there. He asked God, but didn't hear a clear answer. It felt a lot like getting involved in Lacey's life, and that was the last thing he wanted to do. He didn't want involved, he didn't want tangled up. He didn't want to understand her life in St. Louis and what she'd done there.

Pastor Dan walked out of the front of the church, taking the steps two at a time, because that was just Dan. He was always in a hurry to get somewhere. And he was always smiling. Dan had a lot of joy. Joy was as contagious as someone's bad mood, but a lot easier to take. Jay got out of his truck and waited.

"Got business, or are you just here to pass the time?" Dan stopped, still smiling, but with a curious glint in his eyes.

"Passing time." Jay reached into the truck and pulled out two plastic bags with Styrofoam containers. "I doubt she's eaten anything."

And that was the entangled part that he hadn't wanted. He'd noticed her car at the church for the last few hours, and he'd started to think that maybe she hadn't eaten. She wasn't his problem, but his mom had made her their problem. On her way out of town, Wilma had even called and asked him to make sure Lacey was okay.

"I don't think she's eaten since Sunday," Dan admitted. "She's done a lot of praying, though. I would guess that most of it's for other people, not herself. Sometimes life is that way, we can't see the trees for the forest."

Jay pushed the truck door closed. "I'm not sure I'm catching what you mean."

"It's simple, Jay. We look at life, at things that go wrong, and we just see things that went wrong, that didn't go our way. And sometimes they went wrong for the right reason, because God has a better plan."

Jay smiled. "I got dumped for a reason that I don't yet understand."

"Bingo." Pastor Dan gave him a hearty slap on the back. "You'll find Lacey in the youth room. She's mopping, so don't step on the floor. It really irks her if you step on her wet floor."

"Does she work here every week?"

"She volunteers. Our cleaning lady moved and Lacey considers this one of her ministries."

"Has anyone bothered to tell her that God doesn't require works?" He sighed, because he hadn't meant to say the words.

Pastor Dan only laughed. "It isn't about works. It's about love and the works grow from that love, and from her faith. You know that, Jay. When you've gone through what Lacey has gone through, you're a little more appreciative of a new life."

"Maybe so."

"Get that meal in there before it gets cold." Dan nodded to the bags. "Oh, any news on Corry?"

"None."

Pastor Dan shook his head. "I hate that for her."

Jay nodded and headed on up the sidewalk, carrying the meals that were still warm, and telling himself that he was doing what his mom would want him to do. He was taking care of Lacey.

He found Lacey standing in the hall outside the youth room, her hair in a dark auburn ponytail. Her skin glowed, glistening with perspiration.

She turned and smiled at him, the smile hesitant. "Have they found her?"

He shook his head, not surprised by the question. Of course her thoughts were focused on Rachel and Corry. He lifted the bags of food.

"You should eat."

"I'm not hungry."

"I am, and I don't like to eat alone." He handed her one of the bags. "We could sit outside."

"Shouldn't you be at home?"

"My mom is staying in Springfield for a few days. Dad has a pretty serious workload this week and can't make it home, so she's with him."

"You have chores to do at home."

"I'll do them when I get there." He nodded toward the door, amazed that it took so much convincing to get one woman to sit and eat with him. That was a pretty harsh blow to his ego and he'd never thought of himself as prideful.

"People will talk." She continued her objections, but she followed him out the side door to the playground and the pavilion.

"Talk about what?"

"You know, they'll talk about us. I promise you, that isn't what you want."

He sat down on the top of the picnic table and she sat next to him. "It might not be what you want."

She opened the plastic bag and pulled out the container. She lifted the lid and smiled at the club sandwich and fries. "I promise you, Jay, being seen with you could only be good for me. And thank you for this. You either made a good guess, or Jolynn made the sandwich."

"Jolynn." He opened his container. "I asked her what you liked."

She groaned and he glanced sideways. She looked heavenward and shook her head. "Jolynn, she's the main contributor to the rumor mill, bless her heart."

"We'll deal with it." He didn't want to deal with it. Lacey squirted mayo on her plate and dipped a corner of her sandwich into it before she took a bite. He pulled the onions off his burger.

"Thank you for the sandwich." She spoke after a few minutes. Jay nodded. The quiet between them had been nice. He didn't really want to admit it, not even to himself, but she was easy to be around.

"You're welcome. Tell me something, Lacey, why and how do you do it all?"

"Do it all?"

"Work doubles, go to school." He shrugged. "You're going to school, right?"

"I never graduated from high school." She turned a little pink and took another bite of sandwich.

"Okay, work, school, church, the nursing home, cleaning and nursery. Why?"

"Because I…" She looked away, the summer breeze picking up dark hair that had come loose from her ponytail. She brushed it back with nails that were painted dark pink but were chipping at the ends.

She smiled at him. "Because it makes me feel good to be a part of this community."

He didn't buy it.

"I've always tried too hard, too," he admitted. "It isn't easy, being a Blackhorse and knowing people expect a lot from you."

She choked on her last bite of sandwich. As she gasped for air, he handed her a clean napkin. She wiped her eyes and took a deep breath.

"I'm not trying to do anything."

"Okay." But she was.

He sighed and let it go, because he couldn't explain what Lacey didn't want to hear. They were fighting a battle that had already been fought and paying for sins that were already paid for. They were forgetting the grace that covered a multitude of sins.

"Jay, if you want to say something, say it. I'm really tired and not in the mood for games." She looked at him like he really had just fallen off the turnip truck. "What exactly are you trying to tell me?"

"That you don't have to work so hard to be accepted, or worry that God will kick you out of His house."

Her eyes widened and she moved away from him, picking up her empty Styrofoam as she went. "You do know."

"Lacey, that isn't…"

She lifted a hand, a hand that shook. "I don't want to hear it. I don't want to hear what you think of my life or what I've done, or how it was okay. You don't know how I feel."

No, he didn't. He shook his head and she walked away.

Bailey answered the door on the third knock. She opened the door, eyes a little sleepy and blond hair wispy. Lacey shoved trembling hands into her pockets.

"You were sleeping."

"No, I wasn't." Bailey yawned, proof that she had been asleep. "Come in, I could use company."

"Good, because I'm looking for a place to hide." ·

"You've come to the right place. I'm here alone. Cody and our little angel went to a horse auction in Tulsa. They won't be back until tomorrow."

"I don't really want to fall apart in front of Cody and Meg."

"You, fall apart?" Bailey motioned her into the house that she and Cody had built earlier in the spring. They had just moved in last month.

"Me, fall apart, never." Lacey followed her friend into the kitchen and pulled out a bar stool at the island.

"Have they found Corry and Rachel?"

Lacey shook her head. She wrapped her hands around the glass of iced tea that Bailey put on the counter before she sat down across from Lacey.

"Well?"

"Jay knows."

"Knows where they are?"

"Knows about me." She slid her hands up the glass and they came away wet and cold from condensation. "I guess I knew, but I wanted to believe that only the people I wanted to tell would know."

"He won't tell anyone."

"I know he won't." Or did she? She could only remember the look on Lance's face when he learned the truth. He had been shocked and disgusted. Jay had shown pity.

She wanted to cry, because the past couldn't be undone. What she had done couldn't be forgotten. It was in black and white, for anyone to find. She had been arrested for prostitution. It had felt dirty then, and it still felt dirty.

"God forgives, Bailey, I know that. But forgetting and forgiving myself is the real trick. People are so quick to judge, and to walk away. Everyone thinks they know the story and how to fix it."

"I know." Bailey shrugged slim shoulders. "Okay, I don't know. But in a way, I do. I came home from Wyoming pregnant. It wasn't easy, and it obviously couldn't be hidden."

Lacey nodded, because she had met Bailey when Meg was just a baby. The two had become friends because they'd both felt a little lost and alone that first year of Meg's life, and the first year of Lacey's life in Gibson.

"I don't want Jay to look at me the way Lance looked at me."

"He's a different person."

"True, we're not dating and he doesn't feel like I've kept something from him. I should have been honest with Lance from the beginning."

"Maybe, but if he'd loved you, he would have taken time to understand. Just remember, Jay and Lance are two different people."

Lacey smiled, and it wasn't hard to do, not with her best friend sitting next to her. "You can give up the matchmaking, my friend. I'm not going to be the dirty sock in the Blackhorse family's clean sock drawer."

"That's the most absurd statement."

"I like a touch of absurdity from time to time. But you have to admit, it's a fitting analogy."

"It's not. And because you made such a ridiculous statement, you have to make us a salad."

"Bailey, can I really stay in Gibson if everyone finds out the truth?" Lacey looked at her friend, hoping for answers. The thought of leaving left a wound in her heart because this town really was home.

"You can't leave, Lacey. What would we do without you?"

"Make your own salad?"

"See, I'd be lost without you in my life."

Lacey hugged her friend and then hopped down from the stool. "I'll make your salad, but you have to make ranch dressing. That's what friends do for each other."

Her cell phone buzzed. Lacey pulled it out of her pocket and groaned. "It's Jay."

"Answer it."

"I don't want to talk to him. He can leave a voice mail."

Bailey grabbed the phone and flipped it open. "Hi, Jay."

She talked for a minute and then handed the phone to Lacey. She wasn't smiling, and Lacey's heart sank with dread.

"Jay?"

"Lacey, Corry is in Springfield."

"Okay. Where in Springfield? What about Rachel? Are they okay?"

"I'm afraid that's all the news that I have. They haven't caught them."

"Caught them?" She took shallow breaths and sat back down on the stool. "What does that mean?"

"She and her boyfriend robbed a convenience store. Lacey, they had a gun."

"Rachel?"

"I'm sure she's still with them."

Lacey closed her eyes, fighting fear, fighting thoughts that told her that Rachel would be hurt, or worse. She didn't want to think about what this meant for her sister. "They don't know for sure?"

"They don't. Do you want me to come and get you? If you can't drive, I can come over there."

She could drive, of course she could. Her hands shook and she didn't want to think, to let it sink in.

"I can drive myself home. Will you call if you hear something?"

"You know I will."

"Okay." She sobbed a little, not wanting him to hear. "Jay, thank you."

"You're welcome. And I'm sorry."

She closed her phone and slipped it into her pocket. Bailey's hand was on her shoulder. "It'll be okay."

"I don't know how."

"Let Jay drive you home." Bailey sat down across from her, their salads forgotten.

"No, I'm fine. You need to eat. Little Cody Junior can't go without food."

"I'll eat, but you need to let friends help you through this. Lacey, you've always been there for me. Let me be here for you. Let Jay be a friend."

Jay, a friend? It felt like a mismatched shoe. It didn't fit. It was a little tight. A little uncomfortable.

Jay hung up from the call to Lacey and concentrated on driving, on not getting distracted. As he pulled up to the barn, he noticed his parents on the porch. They were home. He hadn't expected that.

His dad greeted him as he got out of the truck.

"I wondered if you were coming home any time soon." Bill Blackhorse smiled and winked, talking the way they had talked to one another a dozen years ago.

"Did you think I would pull a stunt and miss curfew?" Jay smiled back.

"Nah, not really. But as we came through town we saw your truck and Lacey's car at the church."

"I was just doing what Mom asked, making sure Lacey was okay."

"Lacey is a wonderful young woman."

So that's the way this was going. Not that Jay was surprised. His dad had introduced him to Cindy, too.

"Dad, we're neighbors, maybe friends, nothing more."

His dad patted him on the back and they walked into the barn together. "Jay, it's okay to fall in love again."

"Is it, Dad?" Jay pulled his saddle out of the tack room. "I need to work that black mare."

"Working the black mare isn't going to undo what's happening to you. You're letting go. I guess maybe you feel guilty."

Jay shrugged. He faced his dad, and it wasn't comfortable. He wanted to let it go, the way they'd been letting it go for years now.

"Dad, I can't forget Jamie. I can't forget that I loved her."

"No one said you had to forget. But let someone else in. That's all I'm saying."

Jay walked out the back of the barn. At the gate he whistled and the horses, ten of them grazing a few hundred feet away, turned to look at him. A few went back to grazing. He whistled again and they headed in his direction.

"What you're saying is that I should let Lacey in." Jay smiled, glancing at his dad in time to catch a shrug and a little bit of a sheepish look. "Dad, you can't push us together. From what I hear, Lacey is still getting over Lance. I still have a wedding ring in my dresser drawer."

"I'm asking you to pray." Bill reached out to pet his favorite gray mare. "I'm asking you to let God heal your heart. Maybe that's why you came home. Time to face what happened and move forward."

"I think I am moving forward." Time to let go of the girl he loved? He didn't know if he could.

The black mare, Duckie, a strange name for a horse, was at the fence. Jay slid the halter over her head and clipped on the lead rope.

His dad opened the gate and Jay led the mare through, moving fast to keep the other horses from following. Bill closed the gate behind him. A car door closed. Jay led the horse to the barn and tied her.

Lacey walked through the doors, her face a dark silhouette with the setting sun behind her. He heard his dad behind him.

"I'm going to the house." Bill patted him on the shoulder as he walked away, greeting Lacey with a hug.

"I'm sorry. I should have called." Lacey looked a little lost, like she wasn't sure. She stood a few feet from him, from the mare. "She's beautiful."

"You don't have to call." He looked over the mare's neck at the woman leaning against the wall. "You okay?"

"I'm fine. I was on my way home from Bailey's and I realized I really didn't want to go home. There's no one there."

"The police will find her, Lacey."

"And take her to jail."

"They won't take Rachel to jail."

She reached to slide her hand down the neck of the mare. Jay slid the saddle pad into place and then lowered the saddle onto the mare's back. The mare turned to look at him, but she stood still.

"Do you want to ride her?" He tightened the girth strap and knotted it.

"Could I?"

"I think so. I'll show you how to rope."

"No way!"

He smiled and it felt really good. "Yeah way!"

"I'd love it."

It would keep both of their minds off what they didn't want to think about. He didn't want to think about letting go of Jamie. She didn't want to think about her little sister going to jail.

"Come on, we'll take her out to the arena." He led the horse and Lacey walked a short distance away. "You do know how to ride, right?"

"Of course. You can't live around here for six years and not know how to ride."

He laughed because she bristled like an angry cat.

"Let me ride her first and then she's all yours."

Chapter Eight

Lacey felt like a rodeo queen on the back of the black mare. The horse was gaited, so her trot was smooth and easy. Jay stood on the outside of the arena. She kept her eyes focused on the point between the mare's ears and tried not to look at him.

But she did look at him. He smiled and pushed his hat back, crossing his arms over the top rail of the vinyl fence of the arena.

"Bring her over here." He opened the gate and walked through, a rope in his hand. "Here you go."

"You really think I can do this?"

"Why couldn't you?"

"I'm clumsy and uncoordinated."

He laughed again and she wanted him to laugh like that all the time. When he laughed she forgot that her sister was in the biggest trouble of her life, her niece was in danger…no, maybe she didn't forget. It distracted her for a few minutes and the knots in her stomach relaxed a little, but she couldn't forget.

He put the rope in her hand, his hand closing over hers. His hands were strong and warm. He looked up, like that touch meant something, and she couldn't look away, not this time.

She realized she had one more problem she was going to

have to deal with: Jay. Because his smile did something to her heart, shifting what had been numb and cold and for a moment making her believe in something special.

"Here you go." His voice was a little quiet and rough and she wondered if he felt it, too. "Take it like this and make easy loops. Don't work it too hard. You have to look at your target. That's what works for me." He nodded to the horns on a post. "Give it a try and remember, she's going to do some of the work. She knows what to do. Don't panic."

"I won't." If only she could breathe. Breathing would be helpful.

"Relax."

"Okay." She wished. But relaxing was probably going to happen when she managed to rope those horns. Never.

She rode twenty feet out from the target and stopped. The mare responded to her leg pressure; just a squeeze and she came to a halt. Amazing.

"You can get a little farther away," Jay encouraged.

"Umm, no." Lacey smiled and lifted her arm. "I thought it would be easier, and lighter."

"Come on, Lacey, cowgirl up." He winked.

"Okay, here we go." She did it the way she'd seen it in the movies and at rodeos, raising her arm and swinging the rope. It seemed to fly, to soar, and then it dropped.

She never expected it to drop on the mare's head.

But it did. And the mare didn't appreciate it. She sidestepped and jumped back. Lacey fell to the side a little and she felt the horse hunch beneath her, like something about to explode. Lacey had no intention of getting thrown, so she jumped. As she flew through the air, she knew she was hitting the ground face first.

She hit the ground with a brain-jarring thud that rattled her teeth. The hard impact of the ground socked her in the gut and knocked the wind out of her. She tried to draw in a breath and couldn't.

"Lacey, are you okay?" Jay was at her side, kneeling and not hiding his smile the way she would have liked.

"Can't breathe," she whispered.

His smile dissolved. "Does anything feel broken?"

She glared. "Everything."

"Let me help you sit up and you need to take slow, easy breaths. It knocked the wind out of you, but I think you're okay."

"Easy for you to say."

Lacey rolled over and looked up at the sky, and then at Jay. He sat back on his heels and his lips quivered. Lacey laughed a little, but her head hurt and so did her back. Her whole body hurt.

"I don't think I did it." She leaned back again, thinking maybe she'd stay on the ground.

"I think maybe you're not going to be George Strait anytime soon."

"He does rope, doesn't he?"

"Yep."

"I stink. Tell Duckie I'm sorry."

Jay's smile dissolved. "Come on, let me help you up. You sound a little loopy and I want to make sure you're okay."

"I don't sound loopy. I'm fine." She eased herself to a sitting position, aware of his arm around her back and that cinnamon-gum scent.

If she turned he would be close, really close. And being near him upset her balance more than the fall she'd taken.

"You're not fine. That was a hard spill."

"Help me up." She stood, slow and steady, and a little sore. "Nothing broke."

"Jay, is she okay?" Bill stood at the gate. Lacey smiled at Jay's dad and saluted.

"She's fine." Lacey answered. "My pride is hurt. I really thought roping would be easy."

"Come on out here so we can take a look at you."

Jay's arm was around her, holding her close like she mattered. "Why in the world did you jump?" he asked.

"I thought it would be better than being thrown."

Jay and his dad both laughed. Jay shook his head. "Did you really?"

"Yes, I really did. And I was wrong. I can admit that."

"Next time grip her with your legs and hold steady on the reins. She spooked, but she wasn't going to throw you."

"I'll remember that. Stay on horse, don't try to jump. Got it."

Jay's arm tightened around her waist and he pulled her against his side. "Lacey, I haven't smiled…"

And then he was quiet and Lacey didn't know why he didn't smile. But she was glad it was time to go home.

Lacey's phone rang late the next afternoon. She was stiff from the fall and from working all day. As she reached for the phone she grimaced a little. Bailey was sitting at the dining room table and she laughed. But she had promised not to mention the fall again.

"Lacey, they've got Corry in custody."

Lacey closed her eyes. "Okay. What now?"

"I'll pick you up and take you to Springfield. Family Services has Rachel."

"Will they let me have her?"

"We're making phone calls." Jay paused. "It'll work out. I'll be down there in a few minutes."

Lacey hung up and then turned to Bailey. "They have her in custody."

"Jay's taking you to Springfield?"

"He is." Lacey tossed her cell phone in her purse. "I'm scared to death."

"Don't be. This is going to work out. Call me when you get home, so I know you're okay."

Lacey nodded. "I'll call."

Five minutes later Jay's black truck pulled up in front of the house. Lacey had popped a few ibuprofen and she met him at the front door. He stepped out of the truck, leaving his hat behind.

He was the one there for her.

No, not for her. She pushed that thought away, because it was dangerous to her heart. That thought didn't even belong. It was like a kid's activity book, *one of these things doesn't belong.* The thing that didn't belong was Jay Blackhorse in her life.

This was about Corry in trouble, the baby and the police. Jay wasn't in her life. He was...

She wasn't sure and now wasn't the time to deal with suspicion, worrying that he had other motives for helping. She didn't want to get caught up in questions, prodding her to ask why he was involved in her life and what he wanted.

"Call me." Bailey stood behind her. "And stop looking like the sky is falling. That isn't you, Lacey. You're my sunshine friend, not a dark cloud."

Lacey turned and smiled at Bailey, remembering a time when they were on opposite sides of this fence and Lacey had been the optimist. "You're right."

"Ready to go?" Jay stood in her yard, Wrangler jeans, a button-down shirt and his puka-shell necklace. She smiled, because she couldn't help herself. She liked that he had these two sides of his personality.

"I'm ready to go." She smiled when Bailey kissed her cheek. "Thanks, Bay. You mean the world to me."

"Ditto, chick."

Bailey walked down the steps, punching Jay a little on the arm. "Take care of her. She's my best friend."

"Will do." He shifted a little and looked down, his cheeks red.

Lacey pulled her door closed and twisted the knob to make sure it was locked. And then she walked across the lawn with Jay.

It felt worse than a first date.

It was anything but.

"Climb in." Jay opened the passenger-side door and she obeyed, really not seeing the running board, and then falling over it. A strong hand caught her arm from behind and held her steady.

"Very graceful." He said it with a smile that she could hear. "You're two for nothing on the accident scale."

Lacey turned, frowning, and he was still smiling, a smile that showed dazzling teeth and the tiniest dimple in his chin.

"Thanks." She smiled back.

"You're welcome. Do you need help?"

He was teasing and that helped, for a second she forgot the case of nerves that was twisting her insides.

"I'm fine, and you can let go now." She slid into the seat, aware of the place his hand had rested on her arm.

The truck was still running and Casting Crowns played on the CD player, songs of worship, loud and vibrant. She fastened her seatbelt and leaned back, waiting for him to get in. He did, bringing with him that freshly showered and spicy-cologne scent of his.

"Lacey, you have to stop thinking I'm the enemy." He reached to turn the music down. "I'm sorry for knowing about you, about…"

"My record." She looked out the window, watching farmland slip past them. Gentle hills, green fields, a few houses and barns. Not St. Louis, city streets and crowded neighborhoods of people getting by the best way they knew how. Some did better than others.

Lacey's family had been one of the families not making it at all. Never any security or hope, just scraping and trying to survive.

"We've all done things." Jay tried, she knew he really tried. He didn't get it. He couldn't.

"What have you done?" She turned away from the window to look at him. "Well?"

He didn't answer, but he smiled a little smile, keeping his eyes on the road ahead of them. Both hands on the wheel in driver's-ed position. He did everything by the book.

"Did you maybe sneak behind the barn and smoke once, years ago? It made you choke, might have made you sick, and you never tried it again?"

He laughed. "Were you watching?"

"No, but I can picture your skinny little self out there with a friend, sneaking around with your contraband, your little hearts racing, hoping you didn't get caught."

He laughed, and Lacey laughed, too. And it felt good. It felt like a moment of normal in a crazy, mixed-up world. A world that for a time had been on its axis, turning smoothly.

"You picture me as a skinny little kid, huh?"

"You weren't?"

"I was."

"I know. Your mom showed me pictures."

He groaned at that and shook his head. "Of course she did. So you see, we've all done things."

He didn't understand feeling dirty. He didn't know what it meant to walk down the aisle of the Gibson Community Church, wondering if it would be like the other times she had gone to church, wanting to be loved and walking out lonelier than ever.

She closed her eyes, remembering that first week in Gibson, when she'd gone to church and she had gone forward, looking for love. And for the first time, finding it. She found perfect love, and redemption. She found forgiveness.

"Do you know what I learned when I moved to Gibson?" She looked at him and he shook his head, glancing her way only for a second.

"No, what?"

"That the love I had been looking for wasn't real love. I had tried church quite a few times over the years, but I'd had the wrong idea and each time I went, I left unhappy."

"Okay." He waited. She liked that he really listened. He got that from his mom.

"I wanted love from the people in those churches. And when I didn't get the love I needed from them, I left. Not that some of them didn't reach out to me, but they couldn't give me what I needed."

"Forgiveness?"

"Exactly. I needed God's love, and I craved His love, I just didn't know it."

"I know."

"Really?"

He nodded. "I've had my angry moments with God and a few years of wild rebellion because I thought he'd let me down."

"You really were a bad boy?"

"I was."

Lacey looked away, because she didn't know how to go farther with the conversation. She didn't know how to accept that Jay could actually understand her.

They were fifteen miles from Springfield. Jay turned the radio up a few notches and let the conversation go. Lacey was staring out the window. A quick glance and he could see her reflection in the glass, big dark eyes and a mouth that smiled often. But she wasn't smiling. She wasn't crying, either.

She reminded him of a song, a song about a young woman seeking love. And she found it at the cross. Lacey was that song.

"I guess I can't bail her out." She spoke as they drove through the city.

"If you have the money. I don't know how much her bail will be."

"Since she stole my savings, I guess she'll have to spend her time in jail."

"It might do her some good." He didn't want to be harsh. He also didn't want to see Lacey go through this exact same scenario again. And he thought she would if her sister was released.

"I know." Still no tears. "But the baby. I really don't like to think about Rachel being taken from her mother."

"It isn't always the worst thing for a kid." He didn't know what else to say. They'd said pretty much everything on the drive to town. "Lacey, is being with Corry the best thing for Rachel?"

She didn't answer for a long time. Finally she shook her head, but she was still looking out the passenger-side window. "No, it isn't."

He slowed and pulled into a parking lot. "We're here. You can probably see your sister for a few minutes. And then we'll see if we can't get you custody of Rachel."

She turned away from the window, her brown eyes wide. Troubled. "Do you think they won't let me have her?"

"I think they will, but you know that isn't up to me."

"I know."

He parked and neither of them moved to get out. Lacey stared at the police station. Her eyes were a little misty but she didn't cry.

"Okay, let's go." She got out of the truck and he followed.

"Before I picked you up I had one of our county social workers call the family services workers up here. I don't know if that will help, but we can hope."

They walked side by side. Jay's shoulder brushed Lacey's and his fingers touched hers, for only a second. He wondered about holding her hand, but didn't. She didn't need that from him. He didn't believe that she wanted it.

He pulled his hand back and pulled a pack of gum out of his pocket. "Would you like a piece?"

"Please." She took it from him, unwrapping it as they walked. "I don't want to do this."

"It won't be easy."

"Thanks, that makes me feel better."

"Anything to help." He slid the gum back into his pocket. "She's going to try and make you feel guilty."

"It wouldn't be the first time."

"Remember, you haven't done anything wrong."

"Maybe I did." Her voice was soft.

Jay opened the door and she stepped in ahead of him. He took off his hat and breathed in cool air, a sharp contrast from the heat outside. "How did you do anything wrong?"

"I could have taken her with me when I left St. Louis. She might not be going through this." She walked next to him again, her shoes a little squeaky on the tile floor and his boots clicking. "She was about sixteen when I left. She could have been saved."

"You were just a kid." He pointed down the hall. "What were you, about twenty-one or two when you moved to Gibson?"

"Twenty-two."

"You can't keep looking back at all of the things you could have done differently." He stopped at a window and smiled at the woman behind the glass. "We're here to see Corry Gould."

"Oh, yes, just a minute please." She slid the glass closed and talked on the phone. She opened it again and smiled. "Have a seat."

Lacey crossed the room and stood, glancing out the window and not really seeing the view of the city. She sat down next to Jay. The plastic chairs placed them shoulder to shoulder. After a few minutes she got up and walked across the room to look at magazines hanging in a case on the wall.

The door opened. Lacey turned, meeting Jay's gaze first, and then her attention fell on the woman walking through the door. And Rachel.

Lacey choked a little, dropping a magazine back into the rack and hurrying to the woman that held her baby niece. Only a few days, but it had seemed like forever.

"She's a little bit sick." The lady handed Rachel over. "I'm Gwenda Price."

"Thank you, Ms. Price. Thank you so much." Lacey lifted Rachel and held her against her shoulder, feeling the baby's warm, feverish skin. "Is she okay?"

"She probably needs to see a doctor. Her temp is a little high and she's stuffy."

"Okay." Lacey looked up, her gaze locking with Jay's, as it hit home. "I get to take her?"

"We need to fill out some paperwork, and we'll have one of the case workers in your area do a home study."

"What about my sister?" Lacey shifted the baby, who slept through all of the movement.

"I can't answer that question." Ms. Price smiled a little smile. "I'm just here to deliver the baby."

Lacey turned to Jay. He had moved to the window and was speaking in quiet tones to the lady behind the glass. His words didn't carry. Lacey walked a little closer and he turned away from the window, shaking his head.

"Corry doesn't want to see you." He slipped an arm around her waist and she didn't pull away. The comfort of his touch was unexpected. Her need for it, more unexpected. Rachel was cuddled close, smelling clean and powdery, and Jay was strong, his arms hard muscle and able to hold them both.

"What do I do?"

"I think you should concentrate on your niece." He touched Rachel's cheek. "Take her home and do your best for her.

Give her a chance. Corry might come around, if she gets lonely enough."

"I can't do this." Lacey bit down on her lip, her eyes getting misty as she stared at the tiny little girl, now dependent on her for everything. Everything.

"You *can* do this."

"I don't know."

"You do and so do I." Jay moved his arm from her waist and pulled back. He looked down at her, his brown eyes kind and gentle, encouraging her with a smile.

He touched Rachel's hand and little fingers wrapped tight around his thumb. He glanced back up at Lacey and something soft and compelling sparked between them. It had to be her imagination, because Jay was a Blackhorse, and she was the girl from St. Louis that had wandered into town one day.

Jay could hold her close and show compassion. That didn't make him a part of her life. It didn't even make him a friend.

"You can do this, Lacey." He spoke softly.

"I can." She kissed the pink and ivory cheek of her baby niece. "I can."

"You'll have a lot of help. The entire town of Gibson will be behind you."

"Yes, I know."

"We'll need to spend a few minutes talking," Ms. Price reminded, looking at her watch as she spoke. "If you'll come with me."

"Oh, of course." Lacey followed her into a small room, white walls with white tables and bright lights. She glanced back at the door closing behind her. Six, almost seven years in Gibson, and the memories returned full force.

If they'd meant for the room to put someone on the defensive, it worked.

Lacey sat down in the chair Ms. Price indicated, keeping the baby close and praying they wouldn't look at her record and take the baby away. What would she do if she couldn't keep Rachel?

The windows were high on the wall. Ms. Price was between her and the door. Lacey inhaled the cold air of the room, the strong scent of the cleaners used to keep it so white.

"Relax, Lacey, we're not here about you, we're here about your niece. At the moment, you are the person most suited for guardianship." Ms. Price looked over the papers in her folder, glasses perched on the end of her nose. She looked up, smiling. "We would much rather keep the child with a relative. It's easier on them if they're with someone like you, someone familiar, who can provide what they need."

"I can provide. I'll do whatever I can for her."

"Where do you work?"

Lacey gave all of her information. Job, address, income, and even that she was going to school to get her high school diploma. Ms. Price smiled again, her hands sparkling with too many rings and red-painted nails.

"Lacey, you're not on trial." Ms. Price put the paperwork down. "But more than likely we'll have to move toward permanent guardianship if your sister is found guilty. That'll require a court hearing."

"I don't mind." Lacey's heart thumped against her ribs and her lungs felt tight in her chest. "Do I need a lawyer?"

"Not yet. But I would like to know who will be watching Rachel when you're at work."

She hadn't thought that far ahead. "I'm not sure. I mean, I know that I can find someone."

"Is there a day care in Gibson?"

"Yes, there is."

Could she afford it? That was the other problem. All money she'd saved was now gone. She smiled, at Ms. Price, and then at her niece.

"It'll work out, Lacey. There are programs to help you with child care, even with formula and other things you might need. This doesn't have to be a huge burden."

"Thank you. I just want her to have stability."

"That's what we want for her as well. So, you take her home tonight and tomorrow we'll visit with your county workers." Ms. Price stood up. "Do you have everything you need?"

Lacey held Rachel tight and thought of all the things she didn't have, all the things she needed. And she smiled because she had the most important thing. She had her niece.

"We're good."

Chapter Nine

"I don't know how I'll do this." Lacey buckled the baby into the car seat in Jay's truck. He started the truck but didn't say anything. "How can I be the best person for her?"

"Lacey, I can't think of anyone better to take care of her."

She nodded but couldn't look at him, because they both knew what a stretch those words of comfort were. She buckled herself into the passenger side of the truck.

"I need to get medicine for her. I don't know what to give her, though."

"I'll call my dad."

"Thank you."

She touched her niece's tiny hand, warm from the fever. Jay spoke into his cell phone and then he was talking to his dad. She dug around in her purse for paper to write down instructions when he gave them to her.

"Thanks, Dad."

He ended the call and she wondered what it was like, having people to rely on. She brushed aside the thought that could only bring her down. Besides, she had people. She had Bailey, Jolynn and other friends in Gibson that she counted on.

The one thing she didn't have was family that she counted on. No real blood ties that she could call on in an emergency. But Corry had Lacey, and so did Rachel. That was the change Lacey had made in her family. She'd given them someone to call.

She glanced sideways, catching the shadowed profile of the man sitting next to her. It was dark and streetlights glowed orange as they drove through Springfield. And he was the one who had been there for her. She hadn't even had to ask.

"Thank you." She smiled when he glanced at her, his brows raised, a question in his eyes.

"What?"

"For taking me to Springfield. Thank you for this."

"I didn't do anything."

It was that easy for him to shrug off the fact that he'd done something good for her. "You don't get it, do you? I wouldn't have her if you hadn't stepped in. I'm sure they wouldn't have just handed her over to me, not without you backing me up."

He was a Blackhorse. A name did count for something. Good character counted, too. A part of her remembered that she had walked away from her old life and that she'd made the best of her second chance.

Some people change. She thought of the words of a song that sometimes made her cry, because she saw herself in the hollow lives of the people in the words, people at the end of their ropes, hopeless. And then full of hope, knowing that life could be better, they could change. It started on their knees, reaching up to God.

"Lacey, stop being so hard on yourself."

"I guess maybe you're right."

"Of course I'm right." A quick glance in her direction and then his attention went back to the road. "Listen, I haven't walked the straight line my entire life. I know what it's like to live with regrets."

"Really?"

"If you don't already know them, I'm not going to share my sad stories with you. I think life has too many good moments that we miss if we're constantly looking back, thinking about what went wrong."

"So, I'm not the town optimist, you are?"

"If optimism is faith, then I'm pretty optimistic." He pulled into a pharmacy. "If you give me that list, I'll go in and get what you need."

"I can do it."

He was already opening the door. "Let me. I'd rather you stay with the baby."

She remembered that he didn't like to hold babies. He was afraid of them, of their size and his big hands and awkwardness with them. She gave him the list and watched as he walked across the lighted parking lot, long strides, confident.

Rachel cried, eyes blinking and glazed. Lacey spoke to her, stroking her cheek and leaning to kiss her brow. The baby quieted, but her breathing was raspy. Lacey knew how to feed a baby. She knew how to change one.

But a sick baby? This was new territory and her confidence felt like an empty place inside her.

Jay walked across the parking lot, the bottles of fever reducer in a bag with a few chocolate bars. Because he knew one thing about women; chocolate made everything better. He remembered back to chocolate peanut butter fudge made by his mother and Jamie.

He opened the door of the truck, still fighting to let go of memories, and handed the bag to Lacey. When she smiled, he knew he'd done the right thing. He couldn't take it back.

"How is she?" The baby was restless in the seat next to him. He glanced down, smiling at the little girl, at the pretty yellow dress the social worker had dressed her in.

"I'm not sure. I mean, it's probably just a virus, right?"

"I'm not the doctor in the family." He sighed, because those words didn't comfort. "Dad said to take her home, keep her fever down and if you can't keep it down, she should go to the emergency room or urgent care."

"Okay, that does help." She chewed on her bottom lip and looked less than confident. "So, you didn't want to go into the family business?"

"Nope, the medical field wasn't the place for me. Linda is a nurse. Chad is in the navy because he wants to get his medical degree that way."

"It wasn't the thing for you?" Lacey wasn't letting go, he knew she wouldn't. He smiled, because she was tenacious.

"No, it wasn't the thing for me."

"What was the thing for you?"

"I have a counseling degree." He shifted gears, deciding how far to let her into his life. Not far. He didn't want her taking up spaces that were comfortably empty. "I went to the police academy after I finished college."

Her eyes widened a little. He caught the look before he turned his attention back to the road. "Surprised?"

"No, not really."

The tires hummed on the pavement and the road that wound through the country was dark except for the white beams of his headlights and the occasional security light illuminating a farmhouse.

Lacey remained quiet in the seat next to him.

When he pulled up to her house, she didn't move. He turned the engine off and looked at her in the dim light of the truck. Her eyes were closed and her head leaned against the window.

"Lacey."

She jumped a little, rubbed a hand across her eyes and turned to look at him. She smiled a little, embarrassment flitting across her face. "Sorry about that."

"No need to be sorry. You're probably going to need the sleep. What time do you go to work in the morning?"

She groaned and looked at the clock on the dash. "Too early. Six a.m."

"You're going to be tired."

"Yep. But the bigger problem is what will I do with the baby? It's a little late to call around and find a sitter."

"I have to work tomorrow." He didn't know what else to say. He couldn't watch a baby. He wouldn't know the first thing to do with Rachel.

Lacey's soft laughter answered him. She shook her head as she unhooked the infant seat from his truck. "Jay, don't worry, I won't dump the baby on you. I have a feeling that wouldn't be good for either of you. Since she's sick, I'll probably call Jolynn and take tomorrow off. She's probably still up watching TV."

"A day off wouldn't hurt you."

"No, probably not." But he saw her look away, and he knew she was thinking of the money that Corry took. Money she would never get back.

"Let me help you get her inside." He took the infant seat, snapping the handle up.

"You don't have to."

"In a hurry to get rid of me?" He winked as he got out of the truck, and he knew that empty spaces were filling up with this woman, and a baby.

The two were pulling him in. Without meaning to, they were involving him in their lives. He tried to think back, to three years with Cindy and never feeling as if she was really a part of his life.

Because he hadn't really let himself be in hers. He'd kept the empty spaces empty, filled only with old memories that were fading to glimpses of a smile, a soft touch, a scent that brought it all back.

"Jay, are you with me?" Lacey stood next to him, the diaper bag over her shoulder and the bag from the pharmacy in her hand.

"I am." But he wasn't, not really. He smiled and she nodded, letting it go.

"I asked if you wanted a cup of coffee." She swallowed and he wondered about the flicker of doubt, the shadows of what looked like fear in her eyes.

Lacey had empty spaces, too. He had thought of her as the person taking on the world, alone and strong. That was before he'd really known her, before he'd seen beneath the surface.

"I should go." He waited for her to open the front door. She didn't respond.

She opened the door and walked through ahead of him, flipping on lights as she went. It was muggy because the air was turned down. She adjusted the setting on the AC unit and turned back around, her smile, her confidence in place.

He couldn't stay.

She was looking for someone to lean on, to be strong for her. That wasn't him. Not in this house. He'd gone as far as he could, done as much as his heart would allow for tonight.

He realized it was a step forward, in forgetting. A small step, but in his heart he knew that it mattered.

He put the baby down on the couch and Lacey unbuckled her, pulling her from the seat and holding her close. She had given her medicine in the truck. He watched as she kissed the child's cheek, closing her eyes as she held the baby against her.

"Has her fever gone down?"

Lacey nodded. "I think so."

"If you need anything…"

Another Lacey smile, too bright and too confident. "We're fine. And, Jay, I really do appreciate what you did today."

He nodded and walked to the door, Lacey with the baby behind him. "I'll see you tomorrow."

"You don't have to."

"I know that."

He was on the porch and she stood in the doorway, the soft glow of lamplight behind her. And he had a strange urge to lean and kiss her. He took a step back, said good-bye and walked away.

It was much easier that way. Easier to walk away than to get involved and then have someone leave.

Lacey woke as dawn broke across the eastern horizon. She had called Jolynn the previous night and gotten the day off. And more time if she needed it, Jolynn had said. Lacey appreciated it, but she couldn't take more time off. She had today to take care of details. First off, a sitter. And of course, the meeting with Family Services.

She wanted to go back to sleep and put it all off. Maybe another hour of sleep? The baby cried a little and that question was answered. Lacey sat up and looked in the bassinet. Rachel's eyes were open, but watery, and her cheeks were pink, too pink. Lacey touched the baby's face and then leaned to kiss her forehead, the way she'd watched Wilma do in the nursery at church.

"Sweetie, you're burning up." She picked the baby up and walked into the kitchen, where she'd left the medicine.

The chocolate bars were on the counter. Her heart lifted a little, because the gesture had been kind and Jay didn't have to be kind to her. She felt a sharp jab to her conscience, because she had doubted his motives, wondering what he was after when he'd stepped in to help.

Because she had known too many people who only helped when they thought they'd get something in return. Those days were so far in her past, it hurt that the old insecurities sometimes sneaked back in.

She opened the medicine bottle and squeezed the rubber end of the dropper to get the right amount of medicine.

"Okay, Rachel, my dear, time for medicine and then we'll take your temperature." She held the baby in the crook of her arm and squeezed the pink liquid into the tiny mouth.

Rachel fussed, but it was a weak attempt. No smile, no baby grin, no hand reaching for Lacey's hair. "Please God, don't let her be sick."

Lacey lifted her niece and carried her to the living room. She set her down on the couch to take her temperature. And she was right, the fever was high. It hurt, the feeling that she couldn't do anything. She looked at her watch. She'd give the medicine thirty minutes to work.

It was a long thirty minutes. When Lacey took Rachel's temperature the second time, it was higher than the first.

"Baby, baby, what do we do now?" She looked at her watch again, and then picked her niece up. "A damp cloth. We'll try that."

Lacey held a hand towel under lukewarm water and then wrung it out. She carried the baby back into the living room and wiped her bare back and belly. Rachel cried, weak and pitiful.

And then her body stiffened. Lacey froze as her little niece convulsed, her body jerking, her eyes rolling. "No. Rachel, no."

She grabbed the phone and with fingers that shook, dialed 911. Rachel stopped convulsing. Lacey picked her up and held her close, crying silent tears and her heart aching. She couldn't do anything. She was powerless.

And she felt like she was eighteen again, and unable to change her life, the lives of her siblings. Powerless.

"911, what is your emergency?"

"My niece is two months old and she's having seizures."

"Has she had seizures before?"

"No, she has a high fever. I gave her fever reducers, but her temperature is going up."

"What is her condition now?"

"She's sleeping."

"I have a unit on the way and first responders should be there in less than five minutes."

Lacey nodded wordlessly and hung up. She looked at the phone, not sure if the operator had ended the call. She couldn't think about the call, only about her niece.

Rachel slept against her, hot from fever and motionless. But breathing. Lacey heard the sirens of first responders, the community volunteers that always arrived before an ambulance could reach them in the country. She walked to the door, seeing Jay's truck behind the emergency vehicle.

She breathed in deep, her heart letting go of the tightness, just a little. She unlocked the door as the first responders hurried toward the house.

And Jay. Wilma was with him. Lacey's body shook in a sob that she hadn't expected, relief hitting her hard, because she did have people who would come to her aid. She had people.

"What happened?" Jay walked through the door, in his uniform, his jaw set. Wilma took hold of his arm and he breathed in, deep, letting go. And Lacey didn't understand.

The first responder took Rachel from her arms and held her, using a stethoscope to listen to the baby's chest. The other first responder radioed directions to the ambulance. Lacey waited, her body hot and cold, fear holding tight to her heart.

Wilma wrapped a motherly arm around her. "It'll be okay. Now, tell us what happened."

"She has a fever, and I thought it was a virus." She shrugged and let Wilma pull her close. "I thought you were in Springfield?"

"We came home last night. We hadn't planned to, but…" Wilma watched the baby in the arms of the first responder. "Maybe God wanted us at home."

God had known that Lacey would need them.

"She had a convulsion?" The first responder asked. "Her fever is still high. Did you give her something?"

Lacey nodded. "I have it in the kitchen. Do you need it?"

"The amount and time you gave it to her."

Jay stood to the side, motionless, watching the baby. The words of the first responder brought him back to life. "I'll get the medicine."

The ambulance pulling up in front of the house brought a new fear, a new moment of reality. Lacey watched as the paramedics rushed up the steps and Wilma motioned them inside. And then it was a blur of activity, of monitoring the baby and whispered conversations.

"We're going to transport her to Springfield," the paramedic explained. "Do you want to ride with us?"

Lacey nodded. "Please."

Wilma patted her arm and Lacey looked past her, to Jay. He looked away, and she didn't understand. But Wilma took over. "You go, Lacey. I'll follow in my car so I can bring you home."

Jay glanced at his watch and frowned. "I have to be on duty in thirty minutes. I'm sorry…"

This is what distance felt like. She knew this moment, and she couldn't think about it, or why it was happening.

"Don't be. I know you have to go to work. I don't expect…" Lacey let go of the words that would have been harsh and she hadn't meant because she was just glad that he was there at that moment. "You don't have to go with us. We'll be fine."

"Of course we will." Wilma smiled, a little too brightly, a little too big. "Go, Lacey, and don't forget that I'm praying. It's a fever. Sometimes babies have seizures when their temperature gets too high."

"Okay." Lacey breathed in deep, the first deep breath she'd taken in thirty minutes and let it out. She relaxed a little. "I'll see you at the hospital."

Wilma nodded and Lacey followed the paramedics and her tiny niece, just a baby and already going through so much. And Lacey had wanted to change that. She had wanted to make things better for Rachel. She didn't want her niece to grow up in a world that was always chaotic, always full of doubts and questions.

Like her own childhood. Lacey climbed into the back of the ambulance and sat where they told her to sit. She tried to push aside thoughts of being a little girl, of fear in the darkness of her bedroom, her sister and brother cuddled against her sides.

Her years in Gibson had started a healing process. It began with faith, and forgiving. But healing didn't mean forgetting.

But maybe forgetting wasn't necessary. The memories of her childhood provided a backdrop, a place to begin the changes that would make life better. She knew who she didn't want to be.

And she knew what she didn't want for her niece.

As the ambulance pulled away, she saw Wilma in her car, and Jay standing next to his truck, watching them leave.

Chapter Ten

Jay stepped onto the hospital elevator and rode up in silence, people around him talking in quiet tones. One lady laughed at something the man standing next to her said. And Jay couldn't smile, not when he remembered too clearly a trip in this same elevator.

The door slid open. He walked onto the pediatric floor, much the same, but changed. There were murals on the walls now. The bright colors depicted children playing in a park. It was the best the hospital could do for the patients who were here, who couldn't go outside.

They could watch painted children playing in a painted park. They could solve puzzles in a playroom, or watch a clown make animals from balloons.

His stomach tightened into a familiar knot. He stopped at the desk, got a name tag and signed the log-in sheet. The lady behind the desk smiled and buzzed the door for him to enter.

She had given him the room number for Rachel on a slip of paper that he crumpled in his hand without thinking about it. He walked down the hall, breathing in the antiseptic air of the hospital. Oxygen that smelled like medicine. It was cold and clean.

The door to the room was open. He peeked in. Lacey was sitting in a chair, her eyes closed. His mom sat next to the bed where Rachel slept, hooked to IVs. She put a finger to her lips to silence him.

He stepped softly, hoping he wouldn't wake Lacey. As he got closer to the metal crib, he realized that Rachel was awake. Her bright blue eyes were open and clear, not glazed as they had been that morning. She even smiled a little.

"She's much better." Wilma patted the seat next to hers. "But Lacey is worn out. She was up a lot last night, checking Rachel and giving her medicine."

He nodded, but he didn't know what to say. The last few days hadn't been easy for Lacey. He took that back. Since Corry arrived in town, Lacey's life had been turned upside down.

"She's strong," he told his mom. "She'll be fine."

"Even strong people need help." Wilma said it with soft but firm tones that he couldn't argue with.

"I know." He touched his mom's arm. "Why don't you go home? I'll be here for a while."

"Are you sure you don't mind? The doctor said that if Rachel's fever stayed down, he'd let her go home this evening."

"I don't mind." He glanced again at the sleeping Lacey, amazed by the softness of her features when she slept. "Does Bailey know?"

"She came up earlier. So did Pastor Dan and Lillian."

"That's good."

She leaned and kissed his cheek. "I'll see you at home."

He watched her go and then he sat back in the seat, his legs stretched out in front of him, but not relaxed.

Rachel cooed. He reached through the bars of the crib and rubbed her arm softly, careful of the IV. "Little baby, life isn't always easy."

She didn't realize that she'd already found out that life wasn't easy. In her short little life, she'd experienced more than some adults. He prayed that as she got older, it would get easier and she wouldn't have to suffer. If life was fair, she would remain in Lacey's custody where she would be loved and kept safe.

He didn't know Lacey very well, but he knew that she would take care of this little girl. He glanced her way, and she was still sleeping, her mouth open just a little. Street-smart and tough. The description didn't fit her today.

He leaned back in the seat and thought about a girl who hadn't been tough. She'd been sweet and full of faith, with a smile that lit up his day. And she hadn't been able to win her fight.

The memories of losing her were still a sharp ache. Sometimes it felt as though everyone had forgotten but him and her parents, but they'd left years ago.

Jamie hadn't had a chance to become a part of Gibson. She came and left the summer of his twentieth birthday. His mother had brought her to the white farmhouse after his grandparents moved to town. And for a few short months, she'd been a farm girl. The dream of her life.

Lacey moved in the chair, but didn't wake up. She was spending a summer in the country, too. Because she wanted to live on a farm. And because his mother had the habit of bringing home strays.

Lacey and Jamie were nothing alike.

Lacey woke up and the sun was an orange ball on the western horizon. She heard a noise and turned. Wilma was gone. Jay had taken her place in the chair next to the bed. He was sleeping, too.

She stood, stretched and walked to the bed where her niece had been since that morning. Rachel slept, her cheeks pale but not flushed pink with fever. It was a virus, the doctor said, that had gotten out of control. She would be fine, but from this point on, Lacey would have to monitor when Rachel had a fever.

The baby would probably outgrow the seizures, brought on by the high temperature. Lacey lifted her from the bed, careful with the IV.

"Sweet girl," Lacey whispered, and kissed Rachel's cheek. "I'm going to take care of you. You'll never have to wonder what is happening in the other room. You'll never be hungry."

Telling secrets to a baby. Lacey closed her eyes and held her niece close.

The door opened. A nurse, soft shoes, quiet on the floor and a smile that put people at ease. She bit down on her bottom lip when she saw Jay sleeping.

"I came to give you good news." The nurse had a handful of papers that she placed on the table. "You get to take this little girl home. Her temperature has been down all day, she's hydrated, and there's no sign of seizures."

Lacey swallowed objections. How could she tell this nurse that she was afraid to take the baby home? What if she couldn't handle this alone?

Jay moved in his chair, his brown eyes a little sleepy and his hair messy. He ran his hand over his head, smoothing the distracting strands. Lacey met his gaze and he smiled, like she could do it, and she didn't need to be afraid.

She didn't have to handle this alone.

"I don't have my car or the car seat." She didn't look at Jay this time.

"We can give you an infant seat that we give to newborns," the nurse assured her.

"And I can give you a ride home," Jay offered. He stood and stretched, his shirt pulling tight across his chest, and then he shoved his hands into his pockets and waited.

Lacey nodded. "I think we'd rest better at home."

"Of course you would." The nurse removed the IV from Rachel's arm and placed an adhesive strip on the tiny spot.

Rachel didn't cry, but her mouth twisted down and tears welled up in her blue eyes.

Lacey picked her up again and the nurse smiled. "Let me go over the release papers with you." The nurse moved the table in front of Lacey. "And then I'll get the infant seat."

She read the instructions, the doctor's diagnosis and treatment and then she handed Lacey a pen. Lacey held the pen over the area for parent or guardian and the words brought it all home, the significance of what had happened in her life.

She was no longer responsible only for herself. The tiny little person in her arms depended on her, for wise choices, for safety, for nurturing.

And Corry was in jail. Her hand shook as she lifted the pen and signed.

"She'll be okay." The nurse meant the words to encourage, and Lacey nodded. "I'll be right back."

Jay had started packing the diaper bag, a guy in faded jeans and a T-shirt, a man used to being in control and taking care of situations. He didn't look at her.

When he looked up, he smiled. "You're going to be able to do this, Lacey. You're not alone."

She nodded, but couldn't respond. How had he known that she felt alone?

"Do you need anything from the store before we head back to Gibson?" He zipped the diaper bag.

"I'm good."

The door opened again. The nurse walked in, holding up the infant seat. "Found one. And I have some medication for you, with the instructions on the label. She'll need this when you get home."

"Thank you." She had been saying that a lot lately. She buckled her niece in the seat and Jay had the diaper bag. Time to go. She paused, not really wanting to leave the secure environment of the hospital, where people who knew what they were doing were on hand.

"Let's go." Jay reached for the infant seat. "I'll carry her."

"Okay." Lacey said good-bye to the nurse, and followed Jay from the room. She had the diaper bag. He had Rachel in the infant seat.

When they got to the elevator he turned to face her.

"Lacey, it really is okay."

"What if I can't do this?" She asked, not able to look at him, instead studying the pattern in the tile floor. "It was so easy telling my sister what she needed to do. It was easy to help. Now, it's all on me."

She looked up, smiling, because he looked so serious, taking in her words, her rambling fears. Did he ever get riled up, or frightened? Did he ever lose it?

Probably not. He made black-and-white decisions, dealt with facts, and he probably never took chances. He had it all together. Lacey was still not there, and she probably never would be.

For a while she had embraced herself. She was who she was and she was okay. God had done something in her life, was still doing something. But being around him, she felt like her flaws were magnified.

"Come on, Lacey, stop looking like you're about to run out on me." Jay held the door of the open elevator. "Let's go."

"I'm not about to run." She stepped on the elevator ahead of him.

"I didn't think you were. That was just a little well-planned prodding. I figured if I got your hackles up, you'd kick back into gear."

"How sweet of you to think of me."

The sun had set and the sky was a deep lavender with a touch of pink on the western horizon. The sounds were urban and familiar. The hum of city traffic, a siren in the distance and across the parking lot, someone shouted to get the attention of a friend. Lacey breathed in the smell of exhaust and from somewhere, the sweet perfume of a mimosa tree.

Jay held the infant seat in one hand and reached for Lacey's elbow. She followed his lead and he guided her across the parking lot to his truck.

"I'm keeping you from work, or from your horses." She waited for him to unlock the door and set the baby inside his truck.

"You're not keeping me from anything."

"Why are you doing this?"

He set the baby on the seat between them and pulled the seatbelt through to fasten it. When he turned around, he wasn't smiling.

"My mom is paying me."

Lacey opened her mouth, not sure what to say. He laughed. She frowned and stepped away from him. "That was mean."

"How do you think I feel when you question my motives?"

"I'm not trying to insult you, but people tend to have ulterior motives." The words slipped out, more truth than she had planned.

Jay sighed. "Yes, Lacey, people do have motives. I can't deny that you're right. People use others, and they hurt them. But sometimes a guy is being nice, with no ulterior motives. End of story."

A soft spot in her heart latched onto his words, wanting to believe that he really was just a nice guy, and that he might be a friend. She told herself that he'd proven that fact by being there, by helping.

And then that other part of her, the part that had been around a little more, told her that everyone had ulterior motives. He could hurt her. As she doled out more and more trust, he could take that and use it to his own advantage.

She had trusted before. Not just Lance, but other people along the way who had let her down. He wanted her to say she trusted him, she saw it in his eyes, the way he looked at her, waiting. She squeezed the bridge of her nose and tried to think beyond tears, beyond what the moment felt like.

"Lacey, don't make this so difficult." He held the door to the truck and motioned her inside. "You either trust me, or you don't."

"I'm trying." She shrugged. "Jay, you feel like a friend. I hope that's good enough for now."

"That's good enough for now."

Jay didn't know why he had pushed Lacey, or what he wanted her to say to his questions. He started his truck and pulled out of the hospital parking lot, guilt prodding him to apologize. He had pushed her to admit she didn't trust him.

He shouldn't have done that to her. And then he shouldn't have felt so let down when she said he felt like a friend. His ego felt smacked down, like a bad dog chewing shoes. Pete must feel like this on a regular basis.

It wasn't as if Pete really liked shoes. He didn't go looking for shoes. He found them lying around the house and he chewed on them. Jay didn't really like Lacey Gould. Maybe, like she said, she could be a friend.

But he definitely didn't want to step foot into another relationship. He had learned from his failed attempt with Cindy that it wasn't worth it. He had tried to turn a good dating relationship into love, into a marriage.

It had been comfortable.

At least Lacey wasn't comfortable.

"Could we go through a drive-thru?" She had her window down and warm summer air invaded the truck, overwhelming the air conditioner. "I hope you don't mind the window down. After being in the hospital all day, I need fresh air."

"And real food, I bet." He hit his turn signal. "Food, coming right up. What do you want?"

She gave him her order and dug money out of her purse.

"I'm buying."

"I can get it, Jay. You've driven me all over the county the last two days. You've spent two evenings in Springfield because of me."

"It feels a lot like friendship." He winked and then wished he hadn't. "I'm sorry."

"No, don't be. Friendship is a good thing. Who can't use more friends? And really, I'm the one who's being too sensitive."

He ordered and she let him pay. He took that as a move toward the trust she had talked about. She knew that he could buy her dinner and he wasn't expecting anything in return.

They pulled over in the parking lot to eat. Lacey had slipped her shoes off and she ate the burger as if he had bought her steak and lobster. He laughed a little and she gave him a sideways look.

"Can't a girl enjoy a burger and fries?" She shot the comment with a look that put him in his place.

"Of course she can. I just didn't know a girl could be happy with fast food."

"You were hanging with the wrong kind of girls, Blackhorse." And then her cheeks turned pink and she looked away.

"You're right. I did hang out with the wrong women. I almost married one of them." Before Lacey, girls in college, young and flighty, impressed by a cowboy with a wealthy father. They hadn't been looking for long term. He hadn't wanted a long-lasting relationship either.

Until he met Cindy, he had kept the promise he'd whispered on a summer night. Cindy had been comfortable, the opposite of Jamie in so many ways. Come to find out, he hadn't truly wanted forever with Cindy. And neither had she.

"What happened?" She rubbed her cheeks and glanced sideways at him. "Sorry, that's crossing the line."

"No, it's okay. Cindy was a friend and we were comfortable with friendship and with each other."

"Were you in love?"

"Not really. Disillusionment when she turned me down, yes."

"So, you think a woman can't turn you down, cowboy?"

He felt heat crawl up his neck. It was his turn to blush and cringe a little. "That isn't what I meant. I thought we were perfect together. Come to find out, we were just comfortable in our friendship."

"Slick." She laughed. "So, you're not a ladies' man."

"Not at all."

He could laugh now, a little. His heart was healing. Time had taken care of that. He hadn't realized until she'd scoffed at his ring and his proposal that he was moving on.

"Why do you look like she broke your heart, then?"

He finished his soda and shoved it into the bag with her trash, and shrugged. "It's a long story."

"That you don't want to share."

"That I don't want to share." He didn't know why he couldn't. Maybe because he still remembered whispered promises of forever with a girl who didn't have forever.

He had held that summer inside himself along with secrets they had shared. If he talked about Jamie, would she vanish from his memory, be poured out like water from a pitcher and never return? He knew better.

Empty places were filling up. He looked at the little girl in the infant seat next to him. A little girl with a new beginning to her young life.

Something good to pour himself into. And that included Lacey, in ways he hadn't expected.

Chapter Eleven

Lacey rushed to the waitress station at the side of the dining room and refilled the pitcher of water for the third time since the lunch shift had started. A yawn pulled at her jaw and she covered it with her hand. Three days since Rachel came home from the hospital and Lacey was still adjusting to sleepless nights. The baby ate at least twice every night.

"Honey, you look wiped out." Georgia, who had started working the day shift a week ago, rubbed Lacey's back as she scooted through to the coffeepot.

"I am wiped out," Lacey admitted, yawning again. "But I'll adjust. And at least Rachel is feeling better."

"That had to be a frightening thing for you as a new mom."

New mom. Lacey still felt a tingle of fear at the word. She wasn't a mom. She hadn't given birth to this child. She wasn't ready for this, not at all. But instead of the litany of excuses, she smiled.

"It was pretty scary."

"Who's watching the baby?" Georgia turned with the coffeepot.

"Bailey part of the time, Wilma the rest."

"It's good to have friends like that. I had to leave mine in a day care when they were little. It wasn't easy, but you do what you gotta do."

"Yes, I guess so." And a person adjusts when they have to adjust. They learn to live with changes and they learn to take new paths.

She remembered what Pastor Dan had told her: *"Lacey, nothing surprises God. You have to remember, He knew what was ahead of you, and He has a plan to help you deal with it."*

"Hey, you know you've got company at tables two and three."

"I have company?" She peeked and saw the Golden Girls. "Oh goodness!"

"They're a sweet bunch, aren't they?"

"They are, but they're in your section."

Balloons rose from the center of the table and presents were piled up and down the length of it. Someone was having a birthday. Lacey smiled. Those ladies had more fun than any other group of women Lacey knew.

Georgia moved Lacey forward, a hand on her back. "Honey, they're in my section because you're taking a break. This is what we call a baby shower."

"A baby shower?" Lacey planted her feet and tried to stay at the waitress station. Georgia gave her a firm push in the small of her back.

"Get out there, girl. They're having a shower for you and that baby."

"But…"

"Come on, honey, it's time for us to show you we love you." Jolynn came from the kitchen, wiping her hands on a towel. "We put a lot into keeping this a secret and surprising you."

The cowbell clanged and Bailey walked through the door with Wilma and Rachel. Lacey brushed at the tears streaming down her cheeks, because she had people, and they loved her.

These women knew where she'd been and what she'd done, and they loved her.

It made loving herself a little easier.

Bailey brought Rachel to her, and after handing the baby over, she hugged Lacey tight. "Smile, sweetie, this is fun. This is about you and this baby."

"I know." Lacey took the tissue that Jolynn pushed into her hand and she wiped her eyes and then her nose. "I can't believe you all are doing this for me."

Pastor Dan's wife stood from where she'd been sitting with the Golden Girls. "Lacey, you deserve this, honey. We love you. You're such a part of this community and our church. We wanted to do this for you, and for that sweet little girl you're holding."

Lacey held Rachel close and kissed her soft, powdery cheek. And then she realized that her niece was wearing a new dress. The orange-and-pink outfit fit perfectly, unlike some of the baby's other clothes. A little orange bonnet covered her bald head.

"She looks beautiful."

"I dressed her." Bailey pointed her toward a chair that put her in the center of the activity. "Come on, we have games."

"But I really don't need all of this." Lacey sat down, because Bailey was standing behind her, insisting.

"Oh, Lacey, you're going to need all of this and more. You just don't know it yet." Wilma smiled, serene and comforting.

"Here we go." Jolynn passed out paper for a game.

The game took five minutes. Occasionally Jolynn rushed off to take care of customers, and Georgia would excuse herself from time to time. Lacey laughed as the Golden Girls got into the games, laughing and cheering one another.

A memory sneaked up on Lacey; for a brief moment it almost robbed her of this moment. Because she remembered St. Louis six years ago, the summer she left. She remembered a soft cry and empty arms.

"Okay, open the gifts." Bailey stopped the third game before it could start. She shot Lacey a look that asked if she was okay. "I want to see the pretty baby stuff."

Jolynn heard and laughed. "You're wondering if we're going to throw you a surprise shower and what kind of great baby stuff you'll get."

"I definitely want my shower here, with all my friends." Bailey reached for Lacey's hand, giving it a light squeeze. And then she handed Lacey the first gift.

A bouncy seat. Clothes came next, and then diapers, toys and more clothes. Lacey watched as the pile of gifts grew. The last gift was money. She wiped at her eyes as she read the card from an anonymous friend. She looked at Bailey, who shook her head, then looked down, not giving away the identity of that gift-giver.

"You all overwhelm me." She smiled at the group. "I'm so blessed."

"Honey, you've blessed us." Jolynn, hair frosted a light blond and careful makeup hiding her age, smiled big. "You're our kid."

Lacey looked around. The diner had cleared out while the party went on. She stood and looked at the mess left behind. "We should get this cleaned up."

"You can't clean. You're the guest of honor." Elsbeth smiled sweetly. The look she bestowed on Lacey said she meant it and she wouldn't be argued with.

"Look, the law is here."

"Not again," Bailey muttered, and then she laughed, but the laughter was nervous.

Lacey watched Jay's patrol car come to a stop in front of the diner. He got out of the car, tall and yet a little nervous. He glanced around and then he reached into the back of his car.

"Well, what do you know, he's delivering a gift." Elsbeth talked a little under her breath about something in the air.

And Lacey couldn't let them think that the something in the

air was a relationship between herself and Jay Blackhorse. She glanced at Wilma, a woman so giving and kind. Lacey would never hurt Wilma.

It was one thing to throw a shower for Lacey. It was another altogether to have her dating one of the favorite sons of the community. Dirty socks and clean socks. Some things just didn't match.

"Stop looking like a train is about to derail right in front of you." Bailey pinched her arm and Lacey yelped.

"Don't do that."

"You have that look on your face. I know what you're thinking. You're thinking you don't fit. Look around you, Lacey, at the love these people have for you."

"I know."

"You know—" Bailey pulled her aside "—you're stoning yourself. You have to stop doing that and remember what happened when those people wanted to stone that girl. Jesus said for the one who hadn't sinned to cast the first stone. But you're saving people the trouble by stoning yourself."

Lacey looked away from the window, away from the cowboy cop that was walking up to the door. He had caught her eye and smiled, but something on her face must have warned him because his smile faded.

"Stop stoning yourself, Lacey."

Lacey nodded and the cowbell clanged. Jay walked through, a little red-cheeked when all of the ladies smiled and said hello with knowing tones in their voices. Matchmaking was alive and well in Gibson.

"I heard about the shower. I wasn't invited, but I wanted to bring a gift." He held it out to Lacey. Hands trembling, she took the large bag.

Bailey laughed. "Of course you weren't invited. We weren't about to ruin a good time by inviting men."

"Thank you, Jay." Lacey slid her finger under the tape.

"It's clothes." He shrugged. "I hope they're okay. I bought winter things, because I knew that everyone would buy cute summer dresses for a little girl."

Lacey blinked a few times and looked into the bag. A coat, pants, warm dresses and sweaters. She smiled at the man standing in front of her, at ease, army-style, but definitely not at ease in the middle of the women of Gibson.

"Thank you." Lacey took a step back, because he was tall and strong. "They're perfect."

"Good, okay, I have to go." He tipped his hat to the women, and nodded to his mother. "I'll cook tonight, Mom."

A few giggles. He shook his head and explained. "I'm only cooking on the grill."

Lacey wanted to walk him to the door. She wanted to slip her hand into his and pretend she could be the person that someone like Jay Blackhorse loved forever. Because it felt good, watching him walk through a door and knowing his smile was for her.

Even if it was barely friendship.

"Okay then, I think I'll clean up." Jolynn smiled a little too big, a little too bright. "Bailey, help Lacey carry this stuff out to her car, would you? Georgia and I will clean up and then we can all have a cup of coffee and another piece of cake."

Lacey picked up the bags and boxes, and Bailey followed with more bags. As she hit the sidewalk, Lacey stopped to take a deep breath.

"That was awkward." Bailey spoke as the door closed behind them.

"What do you mean?" Lacey walked around to the back of the building and when they reached her car she fumbled to get the door open, dropping a couple of bags in the process.

Bailey laughed a little. "You. Jay. The zing when you look at each other."

"Stop." Lacey turned from shoving bags into the back of her car. "Bailey, it isn't fair. Please don't try to make something happen with him. He's closed off, getting over his girlfriend from Springfield. He's a Blackhorse. I don't want to be rejected again. I don't want to see that look in his eyes, like I'm a mistake that he made one night."

"Lacey, I can't believe you. Do you ever stop to consider what God has done in your life? You act like you're defiled in some way and you can't touch what is clean. And that's crazy."

Words poured out, fireworks of anger, sharp and painful. Bailey ended her tirade, a little breathless and her cheeks tinged with pink. Blond hair blew around her face and she had crossed her arms.

"Okay."

"That's it?" Bailey drew in a deep breath and let it out. *"Okay?"*

"What more can I say? Maybe you're right. I have a lot of hang-ups. I don't want to be hurt again."

"Maybe he'll hurt you, maybe he won't. At least let him be your friend."

Lacey nodded and reached to hug her friend. "I'm okay with friendship."

"You're a lot like Jay. Friendship is safe. It doesn't hurt. God couldn't have planned this any better."

"You're really very funny. I think you should go home to your husband and leave me to take care of this little mess myself."

"Leave, without more cake? You've got to be kidding." Bailey hooked her arm through Lacey's. "Have you heard from Corry?"

"She doesn't want to talk to me."

"She'll come around."

"Maybe, maybe not. I'm afraid. What if something happens and they won't let me keep Rachel?"

"That won't happen. We won't let it."

Jay's truck cruised past. He waved, but he kept on going. Lacey watched until the truck turned and drove out of town.

"Interesting, very interesting." Bailey laughed a little and wouldn't release Lacey's arm.

"Let it go, Bay. You're like a coon dog on the wrong scent."

Jay led the bay gelding into the center aisle of the stable and cross-tied him. The horse shied a little to the left but calmed down when Jay ran a hand down his neck. He touched the horse's front left leg and the animal lifted his hoof off the ground for Jay.

He'd been trimming hooves for the last week, a few horses a night. He'd put off this guy until the end because he was still green and wasn't always so easy to get along with.

"Good boy." He leaned into the horse and filed the hoof. The gelding moved a little, but Jay kept hold of him.

A car drove down the drive and pulled up in front of his mom's house. Lacey. She'd gone home after the baby shower. His mom still had Rachel. If he knew his mom, she'd invite Lacey for dinner. Burgers on the grill, nothing fancy, but at least he didn't add strange seasonings.

The horse shied a little, brushing against him. Jay tapped him on the shoulder to get his attention. "None of that, buddy."

From the drive he could hear Pete woofing, loud and a little frightening. Especially if a person was afraid of dogs.

"Afraid of dogs. Oh, man." He untied the gelding and led him to an empty stall. "Stay there. Not that you have a choice."

Jay hurried out of the barn. Lacey was where he knew she'd be, sitting in her car, windows up. She didn't look happy. Pete looked like he'd just discovered a new favorite game.

"Pete, down," Jay yelled. Pete sat down and waited, but he didn't take his attention off the car. "Pete, to the house."

Pete turned and hurried to the front porch. Lacey opened the car door and got out, not too quickly. She glanced at the dog, and then at him.

"Are you okay?" Jay stopped in front of her, realizing he still had the file. "Need your nails done?"

She sort of smiled. "I don't. But your dog took five years off my life."

"You're going to have to get to know him better."

"Does he dislike all women, or just me?"

"He doesn't dislike anyone." He took her by the hand, a gesture he hadn't intended. But he didn't let go, because her fingers wrapped around his, and it didn't hurt. "Come on, let me introduce the two of you."

"That can wait. Really, I don't want to know him."

He felt her pulling back. He stopped and she stopped.

"You collect dogs." He didn't get it.

"They don't have teeth. They're not real. You understand that, right? Stuffed, porcelain, resin, not real. But Pete, he is real and he has real teeth."

"Once again, I have to remind you that you collect dogs. People typically collect things they like, not things that scare them." He laughed. "They scare you, so you collect them?"

"I got bit when I was five. A neighbor's dog." She lifted the heavy veil of bangs that parted on the left and covered her brow. "I still have the scar."

A jagged line above her brow. He nodded, understanding. "Okay, I get it. But not all dogs bite."

"I know that. I always wanted one and we couldn't have pets in our building. Fear was easier than…"

"Wanting?"

She glanced away from him, and he wanted to turn her, to look into her dark eyes and read the other secrets. But he knew the deepest of her secrets, the guarded past that she tried to hide behind her cheerful waitress persona.

He knew about wanting.

"Pete." He whistled and Pete lumbered off the porch. "Come on, boy, meet our new friend."

Her hand had dropped back to her side, but it slid back into his, seeking, and he tightened his fingers around hers. Pete ambled in their direction, a lumbering red beast with slobber hanging from his mouth, but eyes so kind Jay couldn't imagine anyone being afraid of him.

"He's big."

"He's afraid of the kittens in the barn."

"Kittens? Now that's more like it." She smiled up at him. "Soft, fuzzy kittens?"

"Have you never had a pet?" Jay led her a few steps and when he raised his hand, Pete sat in front of them.

"No, I haven't ever had a pet. Bailey's dog runs in fear of me, because I scared him one time, screaming because he got close to me. Seems silly, doesn't it?"

"Everyone has a fear. Some are big fears, some are small."

"And how do we overcome our fears?" She said it in a soft voice and he didn't have an answer. He feared losing someone again.

He feared forgetting.

It had once been a larger-than-life fear. Now it was subtle, but still clinging to the dark corners of his mind. He shook it off to watch as Lacey conquered her own fear, reaching to touch his dog.

Pete's long, slobbery tongue came out and he slurped her hand and then her arm.

"Disgusting," she said with feeling.

"Yeah, it is." He got the words out, and then he smiled.

"Hey, you two," his mom called from the front porch. "I have the baby asleep in here. Why don't you take Lacey for a ride down by the creek? It wouldn't hurt her to have a break."

Jay waved at his mom, and when he looked at Lacey, her eyes were bright, her smile huge. She wanted to ride a horse. He wanted to sigh.

"You want to go for a ride?"

"Can the dog stay here?"

"Still don't like him?" He nodded at Pete and Pete sat. If only the dog could be trained not to chew up shoes.

"I kind of have a friendship with Bailey's dog now, it's called ignoring one another. So I might start to like him, but let's not push it." She smiled at the dog, his tongue hanging out and his soulful gaze on her. "But he is cute."

"Another nice feature is he's softer than a stuffed animal or a porcelain dog, and he can even keep a person safe at night, or find a lost child."

"He does have positive traits." She reached, her fingers close to the dog's nose, and then she stroked his face. "But he still can't go with us."

"Pete, stay here." This time he did sigh. "Lacey, come with me."

Chapter Twelve

Lacey settled into the saddle of the gray mare. Bailey had taught her to ride, and Lacey never tired of the experience. A horse, a slow canter across a field. She glanced to the side and watched the cowboy who owned the horse as he tightened the girth strap on his big buckskin.

He wore jeans, boots and a plaid shirt. His hat was pulled low over his brow, putting his face in shadow. He turned, smiling at her, but the smile wasn't the real thing. There were shadows in his eyes, too.

He didn't want to take her for this ride.

"Jay, we don't have to do this. Or I could go alone."

He pushed back the brim of his hat and cocked his head to the side. He leaned against the horse, his smile a little soft. "I don't mind, Lacey."

"You look like you mind."

Jay put his foot in the stirrup and swung his right leg over the saddle, settling with ease that came from a lifetime of riding. "It isn't that I mind…"

"Then what?" She loosened the reins and her horse moved next to his, through the open gate and into the empty hay field where red clover bloomed and scented the air with a soft fragrance.

"I'd rather not talk. Let's ride down by the creek. I'll show you the old swimming hole." And he looked away, like there was more to say but he couldn't.

Lacey felt uneasy, like she had invaded private places in his heart, or his life. He didn't want her next door, or riding his horse. He didn't want her in the private places of his life.

"Stop worrying." He rode close to her, close enough she could have reached out to touch him. And she wanted to. She wanted to reach for his hand, to tell him she understood.

Shadows lengthened as they rode. The sun was setting and the creek was in a valley where it was cool and dark, shaded by hills and trees. The temperature dropped and cicadas started their evening song, wings brushing, the sound loud and to some people annoying.

"The cicadas are like crickets on steroids down here." Jay shook his head.

"I love them."

He laughed.

"You would." He had moved a little ahead of her on the trail and he glanced back over his shoulder. "They're not bad."

They rode to the edge of the creek. It widened at a bend and a rope hung from a tree branch that extended over the rippling waters. Jay's horse stopped. Lacey's stopped next to him, no command needed. She watched the cowboy dismount, and then he reached for her horse.

"Come on, we'll walk for a while." He smiled up at her, those shadows still in his eyes.

Lacey slid off the horse, her legs a little wobbly. She reached for the reins that he held and he handed them over, his hand brushing hers, his gaze not wavering, not looking away.

Lacey looked away, because she couldn't catch her breath

and the moment wasn't real, it was created by the creek, the music of cicadas and a cowboy.

Think of something to say, something safe and neutral. She looked at the water, the grassy banks. "I bet you spent a lot of time down here when you were a kid."

"I did. We loved this place."

"We? You and your family?"

"Yes, me and my family." He dropped the reins of his horse and the buckskin lowered his head and seemed to doze. Lacey looked from him to the horse she had been riding.

"You can drop the reins. She'll stay." He took the reins from her hand.

"I'm sure she will, but it scares me to let her go. What if she runs off?"

"We'll walk back to the house and she'll be there waiting for us. But she won't run."

Lacey glanced back; the horse was still standing in the same spot. Jay's hand reached, his fingers taking hers. Lacey's breath caught in her lungs, a combination of fear and expectation.

This felt like falling in love, and she wasn't, couldn't, be falling in love with Jay. It was a moment, just a moment created by a setting sun and soft shadows.

It still felt like falling in love. A lingering ache in her heart reminded her of rejection and what it felt like to not be the woman that a man wanted forever.

"It's a great picnic spot." Jay spoke, his words soft. "I'll bring you down here sometimes. We can bring Rachel."

"That would be nice." Lacey stopped at the edge of the creek, Jay at her side. She looked up and he looked down. And then his head lowered, and she couldn't breathe. Cicadas were singing and a bird dipped over their heads, and she couldn't think, couldn't find a way to tell him no.

His mouth touched hers, their lips connecting. His hands

held her shoulders and then moved to her back. His lips moved to her neck, lingering for a few seconds and she felt his warm breath and a heavy sigh like he felt too much. His lips returned to hers. Lacey closed her eyes and melted into the softness of the moment.

A moment, she reminded herself, so it wouldn't hurt later. It was just a moment.

Jay sighed as he pulled away. "I'm not sure what to think about you, Lacey."

She shrugged and closed her eyes, because she was a *moment*, not a *forever*.

Jay wanted to pull Lacey back into his arms. He wanted to ask why she looked as if her world had come to an end with their kiss. But he wouldn't. If he knew her secrets, she would want to know his.

Memories of Jamie were fading, being replaced by this woman, her smile, her quick wit and her shadows.

He had promised Jamie that he would love her forever, and he would never forget her. At twenty the promise had meant everything. At almost thirty, he realized that it was the promise of a kid to a dying girl who had wanted to feel something that resembled forever.

Jay leaned in again, this time kissing Lacey's cheek, and cupping the back of her head to hold her close, to comfort her. His fingers weaved through soft strands of hair. He saw the tears in her eyes and wanted to bring back her smile. He didn't want to hurt her.

"We should go." She turned away from him and walked back to her horse. Foot in stirrup, she swung into the saddle.

They rode to the house in silence. Jay knew that they were both lost in thoughts they didn't want to share. He stopped his horse next to the barn and dismounted. Lacey stood next to her horse. He took the reins she held. She smiled and she didn't move away. He had kind of expected her to make a run for it.

"Thank you for taking me riding." She reached for the reins of the horse. "Shouldn't we unsaddle them?"

"I'll do it. You go ahead and get Rachel. Tell Mom I'll start the burgers when I come in." He held her gaze, wondering if she had felt the things he'd felt in that kiss. "You're staying for dinner, aren't you?"

"No, I should go home. It's been a really long day."

"I'm cooking," he teased.

She smiled a little. "I know, but I'm about wiped out."

"Lacey, I'm sorry."

"Sorry?"

"The kiss. The ride wasn't supposed to be about that."

That didn't come out the way he had planned. He shook his head, amazed that he could be so dense. From the look on her face, she had to be thinking the same thing.

"Don't worry about it." She let him off the hook too easily and then she walked away.

He led the horses to the barn, his thoughts scrambled inside him. Past and present were colliding. He didn't know how to let go of the one to find the other.

"Why did Lacey look like she was going home to cry?"

His mom's voice. Almost thirty and living at home was not a good plan, he realized. He felt as if he was eighteen again. Jay pulled the saddle off his buckskin and carried it into the tack room. His mom was waiting, her hand on the horse's neck, her other hand holding carrots. Buck took a bite and chewed, his ears pricked forward.

"Do we have to talk about this?" He remembered conversations as a teenager, when he'd poured out his confusion and she had listened, always silent, letting him talk.

Back then he'd thought how great it was, to have that relationship with his parents, when his friends were struggling just to understand growing up.

Today he didn't want to talk about it.

He heard a car. His dad, home from work. That was close, but now he had a way out of this conversation. He smiled a little and his mom shook her head. "I'm not giving up that easily. You were supposed to take her for a ride so she could relax a little, not send her back to me in tears."

"Now you're exaggerating."

She shrugged. "A little."

"Bad matchmaking job, Mom." Did the entire town get together on certain days and plot the futures of single victims? Didn't God have a say in all of this?

"I wouldn't dream of matchmaking." She wiped her hands on her jeans. "Jay, she's a wonderful girl. She isn't Jamie and never will be. And maybe that's a good thing?"

"Maybe." He remembered a kiss that had changed everything. He hadn't thought of Jamie when he kissed Lacey.

"She's been hurt a lot in her life."

"I don't plan on hurting her."

What did he plan? It had seemed easy, to be her friend, to help her in the situation with Corry. That had felt safer than this.

"Jay, you know her past." His mom clicked a lead rope onto the halter of the mare that Lacey had ridden. "I'm not sure if you know how often she's been hurt or how strong she is. Not everyone can come from where she's been and survive it, and still smile."

"I am aware."

"Not everyone can handle where she's been."

"I know that, too." He took the mare and led her to the end of the stable and released her into the field. As he walked back to his mom he glanced in at the gelding he'd planned to work with, whose hooves were half-trimmed. The horse's ears twitched and he chewed on a mouthful of hay.

"I want to make sure." His mom returned to the conversation, not letting it go. "She doesn't have family to look out for her."

"She has you." He smiled at his mom and leaned to kiss her cheek. "I love that you want to take care of everyone."

"And I love you. I love you first, and I want you to be happy." She reached into the stall with the gelding and patted the horse's neck. "You look happier than I've seen you look in a long time."

"I've always been happy."

"No, for a long time you were pretending. You were too young for what you went through with Jamie. If I had known then what I know now, I might not have…"

"Brought her here?" They walked outside and Pete lumbered across the yard to walk with them back to the house. Jay could smell the grill and knew that his dad had started the coals.

"I guess if I could take it back, maybe I wouldn't have brought her, because I would have spared you losing her."

"I don't think we can second-guess. I think we have to accept that God has a plan for all things. And now, I think it's time to find out the next path, the next direction for my life."

"I'm glad you didn't marry Cindy."

"That wouldn't have been God's plan." He could admit that now, and a month ago, he couldn't have. A month ago he had felt rejected. Not brokenhearted.

"No, it would have been wrong. What about Lacey?"

"I've seen her a few times in the last six years and known her for two months. I can't really tell you what I think about Lacey. But she makes me smile."

"That's a start."

It wasn't enough. He knew that. His mother knew it, too. You couldn't build forever on a smile.

The message had been on the answering machine when Lacey got home from Jay's. She was still thinking of the kiss—

trying to decide what it meant—when she learned that her sister wanted to meet with her the next day.

Bailey went with her so she wouldn't be alone. Lacey walked down the hall of the jail facility, Rachel in her arms and Bailey at her side. She kept remembering the voice on the answering machine, young and unsure. Apologizing.

"Do you think she meant it, that she's sorry?"

"Of course she's sorry, Lacey." Bailey hitched her purse over her shoulder, bumping it against her seven-month belly. "She's either truly sorry, repentant, or she's just sorry that it didn't work out. Either way, she's sorry."

"It makes me sick to my stomach."

"Me, too. I want this to all work out for you, and for Rachel. At the same time, I want Corry to find a way to make her own life better."

Without hurting Rachel. Lacey wanted to add those words, but it felt selfish, not compassionate. She had started over in Gibson, running from pain, heartache and guilt. It should work for everyone.

It worked because she had found faith and forgiveness. She had forgiven herself and the people who had hurt her. Even her mom. She'd struggled with that one; her mother had been the hardest to forgive.

"Thank you for coming with me." Lacey handed Rachel to Bailey. "I don't think it will take long. They said visiting times are limited."

Bailey kissed Rachel's pudgy cheek. "We'll be fine. And Lacey, you'll be fine, too. This will all work out."

"I know it will. It isn't easy."

God had a plan. She had to keep telling herself that. Believing had highs and lows. Sometimes it was hard to believe, harder to find faith. But it was there; if she kept searching, she found herself knowing that God was in control. Even of moments like this.

They parted at the waiting room. Lacey followed the female officer to the room where she would talk to her sister. The walls were pale blue, the lights fluorescent. It was like every other jail; it felt cold and it twisted a person's confidence. Even a person from the outside.

Lacey sat down and a moment later the door opened and Corry was there with another female officer. This one stood at the door while Corry took a seat.

Corry looked gaunt and pale, but her hair was clean and her eyes were clear. She wasn't high; she wasn't looking for a fix. Her hands were clasped in front of her on the table and she finally looked up.

"I'm sorry." Two words and then tears streamed down pale cheeks.

Lacey reached for her sister's hands. The guard cleared her throat and Lacey sat back, hands in front of her, like Corry's, but without handcuffs. "I know."

"I want to tell you that I am sorry for what I did to you. And what I did to my baby." Corry sobbed, lowering her face into her hands. "I'm not a bad person."

"I know you're not."

"You know, sometimes I feel like I never had a chance to be good or to do the right thing. I never had a chance. No one ever believed in me." Corry looked up. "Except you."

Lacey nodded, but she couldn't talk. Her throat tightened around the words she wanted to say and her eyes burned as tears surfaced. She had prayed so hard, so often for her sister to have a chance. A few years ago she had even tried to bring Corry back to Gibson with her. Corry hadn't wanted to leave her friends.

"Lacey, please adopt Rachel."

"What?"

"I've been talking to this minister guy that comes here. He

explained your faith, and why you've changed. I never understood. I guess I was jealous. But now, I'm starting to get it, and I know that Rachel needs you."

"You're her mom."

"I'm guilty, Lacey. My lawyer says I'll probably get five or ten years. More likely ten. Rachel doesn't need a mom who went to jail. She needs to be able to go to school and say that she has a mom who works for a diner and has a diploma." She laughed a little. "She needs to have you for a mom and your cowboy boyfriend for a dad."

Normal moments between sisters in an unlikely place. Lacey regretted that it couldn't have happened sooner.

"He isn't my boyfriend."

"You're a little slow, but you'll get it."

"Time's almost up." The voice of the officer.

Corry bit down on her lip and shook her head. "You have to do this, Lacey. I don't have time to argue. You have to be her mom. She can take the place of…"

"Don't."

"No, you're right, she can't. But she needs you, and you need her. I've already signed a paper with my lawyer, giving you custody. Now you have to go and get it legal, so she can be your daughter."

"Oh, Corry."

The officer walked to the table and Corry stood.

"It's the right thing to do, Lacey. For once, I'm doing the right thing." She whispered that she loved Lacey and then the guard led her out.

Lacey cried. She couldn't stop the tears. She couldn't stop the mixture of hurt and joy that mixed inside her heart. Joy, because Corry was finally growing up, pain, because it had to be now, like this.

She left the room and walked down the hall, through security and back to the waiting room where Bailey held Rachel. A month ago Lacey had thought she had life figured out.

Lance had been a wound that was healing, but his rejection had taught her something about herself and it had cemented in her mind that she could make it without a man. She would live her life in Gibson, taking up space in Jolynn's studio and waiting on farmers who came into the Hash-It-Out for coffee and steadily dished-out banter from their waitress.

She had made a plan for herself that included getting her GED and maybe taking college classes because she wanted to be a teacher.

Everything had changed that day Jay walked through the doors of the diner, Corry in the back of his police car, and a baby that needed someone to keep her safe.

"What happened?" Bailey stood, a little slower getting up with a baby on the inside and Rachel holding her hair in both hands.

"I'm not sure." She held her hands out and took Rachel. Bailey had to untangle baby fingers from her hair.

"You're not sure."

"She wants me to adopt Rachel. She wants her baby to have someone who will make the right decisions for her, and give her a chance." Lacey held her niece close. "What if I'm not that person?"

Bailey walked next to her, down the hall and out into bright sunshine and heat. "Of course you're the right person. And you can give her something else that Corry couldn't. You give her community and people who love her. You give her stability."

"I know you're right, but it isn't the perfect plan, is it? The perfect plan would include Corry getting her life together and making the right decisions."

"That isn't going to happen right now. And right now is what needs to be taken care of."

"I guess you're right." Lacey unlocked her car and Bailey opened the back door so she could put the baby in the car seat.

"Of course I'm right." Bailey spoke with a soft smile. "Remember, when we're giving each other words of wisdom, we're always right."

"Of course, how could I have forgotten?"

"Momentary lapse." Bailey buckled her seat belt. "Lacey, it'll all work out."

"I know it will. It's a little scary at the moment, but I know it'll work out."

It was still early. Her mind turned to easier thoughts: a day off and weeding her flower gardens. But somehow Jay entered into those thoughts, because lately he had done that a lot.

No matter how much she told herself it was wrong, that it wouldn't work, her silly heart still insisted on thinking about him and what it felt like to be held in his arms.

No one had ever made her feel as safe, or as threatened.

Chapter Thirteen

Jay walked out of the barn and looked toward the old farmhouse. Lacey's sedan was back. His mom had told him that Lacey went to see Corry. He had wondered about the meeting, and worried. He knew that Lacey could hold her own, but he worried that Corry would manipulate her.

The movement of the mare inside the barn drew him back inside, into the dark interior that smelled like hay and horses. A cat ran past him, chasing a mouse that ran up a post. The horse turned, her sides heaving and her head down.

"It won't be long, Lady." He leaned his arms on the top of the gate. The horse looked up, eyes sad, and then she turned again. Away from him.

She would have the foal any time. But she didn't appreciate his presence. He walked back to the door, to sunlight and heat. It felt good to take his hat off. There wasn't much of a breeze but enough. At least the mare had the fan that he had plugged in and hung outside her stall.

"Be back in a little while. Don't have the baby while I'r gone." He looked back inside. The horse didn't seem to car that he was leaving.

Lacey would probably love to watch the mare give birth. He had a feeling she was all about newborns. He walked to his truck and jumped in, starting it with the key that he never took out of the ignition. He should; it wasn't as if Gibson was completely crime-free. But they didn't have a lot of car thefts in the area.

When he pulled behind her car and parked, he saw her weeding flower gardens that hadn't been taken care of in a couple of years. The last renter hadn't been interested. And then the house had been empty for a year.

He got out of his truck and walked across the yard. A playpen was set up in the shade of a big oak tree. Next to it, Pete. So that's where the dog had gone off to. Jay shook his head and gave his dog a look. It didn't do any good. Pete looked pretty happy with his spot under the tree. And he had a rawhide bone.

"Looks like you have company." He spoke as he walked up behind Lacey. She jumped a little and turned.

"Don't do that."

"Sorry. I thought you heard me."

"I did, but I didn't realize you were behind me already." She pulled off gardening gloves and brushed hair back from her face. Somewhere along the way she had gone from cute to beautiful. Maybe it was her smile, or the way her eyes lit up.

He was as confused as Pete obviously was. He shook his head. "Sorry. I came down to see if you wanted to watch my mare give birth. It'll probably happen in the next couple of hours."

"I'd love to watch."

"How did it go with Corry?"

She glanced at the baby in the playpen, holding a rattle and cooing. "She wants me to adopt the baby. She's been meeting with a minister and she's decided Rachel should have stability. With me."

She looked away, cheeks flushed. He wondered, but didn't know how much to ask, about what this meant to her.

"I'm going to do it." She pulled a weed, continuing to talk, but not looking at him. She moved a little and pulled crabgrass that was spreading through the flowers.

"You'll be a great mom."

"I hope. I don't know."

"Lacey, I don't get it. This seems like an easy decision to make. Actually, I can't imagine that it would really require a decision. Do you not want her?"

She leaned back on her heels and looked up at him.

"Of course I want her. I want her more than anything. I'm just afraid. And I don't want to make mistakes with her life."

"I think my mom would tell you that every parent makes mistakes. And I'm telling you, that little girl will be better off with you. And Corry knows it. So stop worrying."

She nodded a little, biting down on her lip, the pulled crabgrass still in her hand. "Jay, I had a baby."

He stared, too surprised to say anything. He kneeled next to her, reaching for a dandelion. She slapped his hands away.

"Not the dandelions." The words caught on a sob.

"What?" It didn't make sense. They were talking about babies, not dandelions.

"The dandelions are my favorite flowers."

"They're weeds." He wanted to talk about babies and the stark sadness in her eyes, the loss. He could tell her that he knew how it felt, to let go of someone.

"They're not weeds. They're sunny, happy flowers and I love them. People are always trying to get rid of them, yanking them out by the roots and tossing them. But they survive because God designed them with a purpose. He made them strong." Tears rolled down her cheeks.

"Strong, like you."

She wiped at her eyes. "I don't feel strong. Dandelions are survivors. They can grow anywhere. They fill up bare places."

Filling up bare places. He sighed, because she was a dandelion and she didn't know it. He didn't know how to tell her that, or what to say about a baby she had given up.

She smiled up at him, tears clinging to dark lashes, smearing liner under her eyes. "Did you know dandelions have a lot of vitamin A?"

"I see. That's probably why my grandmother wilted dandelion greens with bacon grease and made me eat them every summer." Jay reached for hands that were busy pulling weeds while tears fell. "Lacey, I'm sorry."

She nodded, tears sliding down her cheeks and dropping onto the dry earth. Sad tears watering her dandelions.

"I gave her up for adoption. I knew that I wasn't prepared to be a mother, not the mother she needed. So a family in Ohio adopted her."

"You gave her life. That's an amazing thing. It isn't always the choice that a woman makes when she feels like her back is against the wall."

"I wanted her to have life, and to have a life with a family that loves her and takes care of her. Everything I never had and couldn't give her. And now Corry thinks I can give her daughter that life."

"I believe you can, too."

"I'm single. I work at a diner and live on tips."

He wanted to tell her he would help, but he couldn't. He had already done that once, proposed because it seemed like the thing to do. He had actually proposed twice. The first had been accepted.

"You have people who will help you, Lacey. You can do this."

She looked up, eyes red and tears trickling down her cheeks. He wiped the tears away, and then he kissed her, because it felt like the thing to do. She was looking at him as though she believed it when he said she could raise Rachel.

She kissed him back, soft and easy like a spring day, and then she moved, out of his embrace and out of his reach.

"You have to stop doing that. You're confusing me. We're friends, and then you kiss me like that. I don't want to be this woman that you kiss when the moment feels vulnerable. I'm not…" She stood up. "I'm better than that."

He stood next to her. "Yes, you are, and I'm sorry. I didn't mean to hurt you."

"Why can't life be simple? Why couldn't I have been the girl who grew up in this town, making the right choices and living the life I wanted?"

"Because life isn't predictable and we all have a path. What we go through makes us who we are. And now God is replacing what you lost, with Rachel."

Replacing what was lost. He faltered at those words and looked away from Lacey, to the fields and the distant stable. He needed to escape the sweet tangle that was Lacey Gould.

"Let me get Rachel." Lacey dropped her gardening shovel and gloves into the nearby wheelbarrow. "I still want to see that baby horse."

No way out. He smiled and walked across the yard with her. He watched as she gathered the baby and her bag. She pointed to the playpen.

"Can you grab that?"

"I can." He folded it, or at least he figured it out after two or three tries. Lacey stood next to him, smiling again. It didn't take her long to bounce back.

"Let's go." He walked back to the truck and as he stowed the playpen in the back and lowered the tailgate for Pete to jump in, she strapped the baby into the car seat she'd pulled out of her car.

She'd make a good mom.

Lacey loved the stable, with the dust, the smell of hay, horses moving restlessly in their stalls and the cats climbing around, looking for mice. It felt like a comfortable place that a kid could have hidden in while playing hide-and-seek.

She asked Jay if he had played there as a kid.

"We did. Linda, Chad, me and a few neighbor kids would hang out in the barn. It wasn't this barn, not back then."

Lacey closed her eyes, remembering her own childhood, riding bikes down busy streets and staying away from her mom as much as possible. That had been a game of hide-and-seek she would have gladly not played.

She was a whole person, though. And happy. She looked at the baby sleeping in the playpen, the dog on the ground next to her. He'd taken up the job of protector. Lacey smiled. Jay, in the lawn chair next to hers, moved.

They were sitting in a stall opposite the stall where the mare was laboring. Jay stood and walked out into the aisle. He came back shaking his head.

"She's stubborn."

"I'm not sure why you're watching her. Won't she give birth on her own?"

"She will, but this is her first foal and we've only had the mare a month. I bought her at the auction."

"At the auction?"

"She was cheap and I was bidding against guys that wouldn't have taken her to a nice home. She's part Arabian and sometimes they have thicker placenta and the babies need help breaking through the sac. Especially if she's been on a fescue-grass diet."

"That's a lot to remember."

"It's all information you pick up as you go. Sometimes you pick it up through a bad experience."

"A lot like life."

"I guess. Yes."

Pete lifted his head and looked at the wide open doors of the barn. Wilma Blackhorse walked through the opening, her smile wide. "There you two are."

"We're waiting for Lady to have her foal." Jay got out of his chair and motioned for his mom to sit.

"I wanted to see if you need anything." Wilma glanced in the direction of the baby, her smile soft. "I thought I might see if Lacey wants me to take the baby to the house."

"Are you sure?" Lacey had to ask. "I don't want you to feel like you have to constantly watch her."

"Lacey, I love you and that baby. Remember, I have a grandchild that lives hundreds of miles away that I can't see or hold every day."

Wilma was already gathering baby stuff. Lacey lifted the infant from the playpen, kissing her cheek before handing her over to Wilma.

"Now, we'll just go on up to the nice, cool house and you two stay and make sure that foal is safe." Wilma smiled as she walked out the barn door, holding Rachel close and talking to her.

Lacey watched them go, watched the horse, watched cats playing and finally sat down. Jay sat next to her. Neither of them talked. Lacey avoided looking at the man next to her, because he had to know that his mom was starting to think of them as a likely match.

"She's never been subtle." Jay finally spoke, legs stretched in front of him, his jeans bunched over boots that were scuffed.

Lacey looked down at her worn sneakers, dirty from gardening. She tried not to think of all the differences between them.

"She means well. She just doesn't understand."

Jay looked at her, eyes narrowed. "What?"

"Me, the girl next door who is anything but the girl next door. Jay, I'm not naive. I know that I'm not the type of woman a man thinks of when he thinks of a wife and mother for his children."

"You're selling yourself short, Lacey. I'm not interested in a relationship with anyone. If I was…"

She waited, wondering for a moment why she was holding her breath, why she wanted to hear him say something that would make a difference. When she looked into Jay's eyes, she saw acceptance. And he knew all of her secrets.

"Lacey, I'm not ready to share deep, dark secrets. Maybe because I'm a man and we're not geared to talk about our feelings—" he flashed a cowboy grin and wink that lightened the moment "—but I couldn't imagine being ashamed to take you home to meet my family."

"You know that I dated Lance?"

"I know."

"I'm over him. I'm over whatever was between us. I'm getting over being rejected and dealing with the reality that he thought it was okay to date me, but all of our dates were in Springfield and never here, where people could see."

"Maybe it's time for you to forgive yourself."

"What?"

"You're still holding on to what you did in St. Louis. You're still punishing yourself and telling yourself you can't have what other people have because you made mistakes."

Lacey looked away from questioning eyes that were warm and compassionate. "I know. But Jay, people don't always let go of what they know about someone. I sold myself, and in the process I lost part of my self-worth. It isn't always easy to look in the mirror. It isn't easy to feel clean when for so long I felt dirty."

"You've asked for forgiveness. Maybe it's time to forgive yourself and to realize no one is perfect or sin-free."

Lacey nodded, because he made her want to believe in herself, but she couldn't tell him that. She couldn't take that step into his life and make a connection that would only lead to a broken heart.

Movement from the stall across from them brought both out of their seats. Jay walked to the stall and Lacey followed. Neither of them spoke.

The mare moved to the corner of the stall, head down. Lacey held her breath, watching as the foal slipped to the ground, dark and slimy on the straw-covered floor. Jay opened the stall door and moved quietly, talking to the mare. He helped the mother free her baby from the sac that covered its body. He used a towel to wipe the face, the nose and ears. When he stepped back, the mare took over, cleaning the dark, still-wet baby.

"It's a girl." He smiled over his shoulder, but the smile didn't reach his eyes.

"Jay, I'm sorry. I don't want things between us to be complicated." She shrugged. "I like having you for a friend."

He nodded and stepped back to lean against the wall. He draped the dirty towel over the gate and his gaze remained on the mare and foal.

"Lacey, I just got out of a relationship. It took me three years and a rejection to realize it would have been a mistake. I didn't love Cindy. She was easy to be around." He turned to Lacey, his brown eyes serious, his smile gone. "I won't do that to another woman. It isn't fair to slide into another relationship because it is easy."

"You don't have to explain."

"That isn't an explanation. It's a fact, and it's hard for a man to admit he nearly messed up someone else's life to make his own a little easier."

"I can't picture you looking for an easy relationship. You've got a big house nearly framed, a good life here, and it seems like you'd want to fill that life with a wife and kids."

"It seems that way, doesn't it?" He moved out of the stall door and stood next to her, resting his arms on the door. His shoulder brushed hers. "I'll tell you all about it someday."

"Okay."

Lacey focused on mother and baby. The little foal, still too wet to tell her true color, tried to stand again. She would get up on hind legs, front legs still bent, and push. And down she'd go. The mother horse nuzzled her, encouraging her to try again.

It took a few minutes. Finally, on wobbly legs, she stood next to her mother.

"She's beautiful." Lacey leaned, looking in at the most miraculous event of her life.

"I'm going to name her Dandelion." Jay winked as he spoke. "And when she's weaned, she's yours."

"Jay, I can't take a horse."

"She's a gift. Lacey, I bought her mom for almost nothing, just to save her life. The baby was a bonus. She's yours. Just call her Dandelion, okay?"

"Dandy for short."

"Okay." He stepped out of the stall. "And don't let the Gibson matchmakers bother you too much. They've been at it for years. Probably for decades. A long time ago they wanted me to marry Bailey. Think about what a mistake that would have been."

A mistake. She nodded and let her gaze drift back to the mare and her foal. Lacey didn't want to be anyone's mistake.

"I should go." She stepped back, not really wanting to leave the mare and the little filly, Dandelion.

"Don't." Jay remained next to her. "Lacey, I have stories, too. I'm just not ready to share."

"You don't have to share." She folded the playpen, smiling a little because Jay watched, shaking his head like he had more to say.

"You make that look easy." He meant the playpen, she knew.

"Practice." She carried the playpen out of the stall they'd been sitting in and he took it from her.

"You can't walk home with all of this stuff and the baby."

She groaned, because she hadn't thought of that. She had ridden down in his truck. And she had the baby. It was no longer just her, taking care of herself.

"I'll get Rachel." She let him take the playpen from her hands. In some circles this would have been running away. Maybe it was. She didn't want to hear personal stories that would lead her further into his life, and she didn't want to be anyone's mistake.

Chapter Fourteen

Three days after a foal named Dandelion was born and she'd learned that Jay had secrets, secrets Lacey didn't want to know, she stood on the porch and watched the county social worker drive away. Lacey felt a little sick to her stomach, not knowing what the lady had meant by *hmmm* and *um-hmmm*.

As her car pulled away, Bailey's pulled in. Lacey let out a sigh of relief that only Pete heard. Pete. She still didn't love the dog, but he was growing on her. She looked at him, frowning a little, a gesture he obviously didn't get. His tail thumped the wood porch.

"Was that the case worker?" Bailey walked up to the porch. "And isn't that Jay's dog?"

"It is Jay's dog, and yes, it was the case worker. She did the home study."

"How'd it go?" Bailey glanced at the dog again and shook her head. "Why is Pete here? You don't like dogs."

"He's a little like his owner, kind of clueless sometimes."

"Jay, clueless?" Bailey walked into the semi-cool interior of the house. "I love this place."

"Me too." She led Bailey to the kitchen. "Thank you for watching her tonight."

"I don't want you to quit school."

"Again." Lacey turned and smiled as she pulled a pitcher of lemonade out of the fridge. "Want some?"

"Homemade?"

"Of course."

Bailey nodded and got glasses out of the cabinet. "So, Jay is clueless?"

"Of course he is. We have this strange friendship that only exists because he brought Corry to the diner and I moved in here. He didn't want that, but now we're friends and I don't know."

"He's drop-dead…"

"Stop." *Gorgeous* wasn't a word that Lacey needed supplied in order to picture the cowboy with the dark hair and stomach-tilting smile.

"Okay, I'll stop. So, his dog likes you."

They sat down at the table. Lacey pushed a plate of cookies to her friend. Bailey took one, and then took another.

"Yes, his dog likes me." Lacey smiled at the baby sleeping in the playpen. "And I like Jay. As a friend. As a neighbor."

"I'm glad to hear you're opening that door."

After a drink of tart and sweet lemonade, Lacey explained, "I told him about my little girl."

Bailey's eyes watered and a few tears spilled out. That hadn't been Lacey's goal. Tears should be behind them.

"Oh, Lace, I'm sorry. I know this can't be easy for you, with Rachel and the memories."

"It's easier than I thought it would be. It's been years, and I'm a different person. And that little girl has a life with a family that loves her. It's the way it's supposed to be." She smiled. "I never thought I'd be able to say that."

"So then, what's the problem with Jay?"

"I'm okay with my past. I don't want for someone else to have to be okay with it."

"I guess that make sense."

"Not only that, but I don't want to be his rebound girl. He got rejected by someone he dated for three years. That has to leave a few wounds."

"He wasn't in love with her. *She* was the rebound girl."

"He told me he wasn't in love with her, but that's all I got from him."

"You don't know about Jamie?"

"I guess not."

"She lived here. In this house."

Lacey closed her eyes. "Wonderful. Now I understand why he didn't want me here."

"They were—"

Lacey raised her hand. "I don't think I want to hear this."

"She came here—"

Lacey stopped her friend. "Bailey, I mean it, I don't want to hear. This is his story, and I don't want his story. I don't want to hear his secrets. I don't want to be connected to him that way. I don't want…"

"To have your heart broken?"

She nodded. "I don't want to fall in love with him, because I'm fine the way I am. I have Rachel now. I love this town and I love my friends here. It's taken me a long time to get to this place."

"You're absolutely right, you have made it. You're a bigger part of Gibson than you realize."

"I know, but I guess I'm always waiting for the floor to drop out from under me. It only takes one person bringing it up, making a big deal of it, and then people start to talk."

"True, but you're a part of this community now. Lacey,

people know you and love you. Everyone gets talked about, people do gossip, but there are more people who love you than who would want to hurt you."

"You can be right about that." Lacey smiled, and it was easier to smile now. "But I'm right about relationships."

"Okay, if that's the way you want to play, I'll let you be right about relationships. I get to be right about everything else."

"Deal." Lacey looked down at her watch. "And if I don't get going, I'm going to be late for class."

"Go. We'll be fine. Oh, did you talk to the lawyer?"

"Yep. We have to go to court and have a judge approve everything." She reached for her books. "As long as the home study comes back okay and no one contests the adoption."

"It will work out."

"Bailey, I want to be an optimist, but I have to be realistic on this. I have a record. What happens if they don't approve me for this adoption?"

"We'll make sure she stays here."

"How?"

"Cody and I will adopt her."

Lacey hugged her friend for that out-of-character impulsiveness. "I love you, Bailey. See you later."

Lacey hurried to her car, trying not to look at the truck that drove past, or the cowboy who waved without really looking in her direction.

Jay reached for his phone the next morning. Without thinking his plan through, he dialed Lacey's number, knowing she was up, even after her late night at school.

He'd made the mistake of stopping by Lacey's the night before, and he'd gotten stuck talking to Bailey.

Bailey, who had questioned him about his intentions toward her friend. He had to smile at the protectiveness that had been evident. He didn't plan on hurting Lacey. He had told Bailey that he didn't have *intentions*.

She answered on the third ring, a little out of breath, her voice soft.

"Lacey, are you busy?"

"No, why? Is everything okay?"

He sat down in the rocking chair on his mom's front porch and watched as the construction crew worked on the roof of his new house. "Everything is fine. I just thought I'd see if you wanted to go riding."

"I don't know." Hesitation. "Jay, what's going on?"

"They did the home study yesterday. I thought you might need to be distracted."

"Thank you."

"So, riding?"

"I want to be here when they call, so I really can't go riding."

"How about if I come down there. We can water the dandelions."

"That isn't nice, making fun of a girl because she shared something with you."

"You're right. So, how about a picnic and Pete can play with Rachel."

"A play date with the kids, how fun." Her tone teased and he smiled. It sounded like a normal conversation between a man and a woman. Then Jay knew that he shouldn't have called.

Too late now. She was silent on the other end, waiting for him to say something.

"Yes, a play date."

"Come on down."

Jay drove down to Lacey's with a picnic basket on the seat next to him and Pete in the back of the truck. When he pulled up to Lacey's she was sitting in the backyard on a canopy-shaded swing. The baby was sitting in her lap.

He got out, Pete hurrying ahead of him. The dog sat at Lacey's feet, nuzzling her hand and then sniffing the baby. Jay reached them, smiling a little because they were quite a trio, that dog, the baby and Lacey.

He wasn't sure where he fit in. That thought didn't make sense. He wasn't supposed to fit in here.

"Have you heard from the lawyer?"

She shook her head, standing with the baby. "Not yet. I'm a little nervous."

She handed him the baby girl. In the short time Rachel had been at Lacey's she'd grown and she smiled more. Drool slid down her chin and she touched his cheek with her tiny hand.

"She likes you." Lacey took the picnic basket.

"Good thing she doesn't know that I'm scared to death of her."

"Good thing. But I think babies are like dogs. They smell fear." Lacey pulled a cloth off her shoulder and wiped the drool off the baby's chin. "What's in the basket?"

"Chick food."

"Chick food?" Her brows arched and he thought that she was spunky and beautiful. The rough edges he used to imagine had softened and her smile teased.

"The kind of food women like. It usually contains nuts and fruit."

"Is that the definition in Webster's?"

"It's the Jay definition." He kissed Rachel's cheek and then looked at Lacey. "Chicken salad, croissants, salad with some kind of fruity-tasting dressing and cheesecake."

"Wow, it *is* chick food."

"Mom bought it at some *homemade but not* deli in Springfield."

"You're willing to eat such chick food? For me?"

"For you."

She turned a little pink and he didn't comment. He felt as if the picnic mattered in ways he couldn't begin to understand.

"I'm going to take it in the house for now." Lacey stepped back, away from him and the baby. "You hold Rachel. I'll put this in the fridge. The last thing we need is food poisoning. And I'll make lemonade."

He smiled because she was rambling.

"I'll sit here in the shade with Miss Rachel." He watched Lacey go and then he sat down on the swing, the baby in his arms, her fingers wrapping around his, and she cooed.

"Little girl, you are one special creature. You know, I think your aunt is special, too. Don't tell her that." He leaned back, the baby sort of standing in his lap, her slobbery mouth on his shoulder. "It isn't easy, moving forward. It isn't easy to let go of promises."

He sat Rachel back on his lap and she gave him a crooked grin. "Yes, like you know exactly what I mean. It's easy to tell you secrets. Who are you going to tell?"

The baby blew spit bubbles and he lifted her to kiss her cheek. "I know exactly what you mean. Life is definitely complicated."

She grinned again, and then her face turned red and she made another face. "Oh, well, that's not pleasant."

He looked from the baby to the house. No sign of Lacey. He held the baby out a little and wrinkled his own nose. Rachel smiled, obviously thinking his face was part of a game to entertain her.

The back door slammed shut. Pete got up and walked away, choosing a place under the shade tree. Lacey laughed as she crossed the yard. "Is she suddenly toxic?"

He nodded and held the baby out to Lacey. "I think she is."

Lacey took her niece and held her, not bothered, obviously. "I'll change her and be right back. Try not to look so offended."

He laughed a little. "You have to admit, it isn't nice."

"I admit, it really isn't. But you're a country boy, you've seen worse."

"I'm not sure if I've smelled worse."

* * *

Lacey walked through the back door, Rachel cooing against her shoulder, and smelling really unpleasant. She put the baby down on the changing table in the tiny spare bedroom and reached for the diapers. The phone rang.

Of course it would ring while her hands were full with a messy baby, diapers and wipes. She held Rachel and reached for the phone, knocking the wipes off the table in the process.

Footsteps on the floor in the kitchen. She turned as Jay walked into the room, and she answered the phone.

"Miss Gould, this is Lynette McCullough from Family Services. I wanted to let you know that the review for your home study was positive and we can proceed with the adoption. We'll go to court in two weeks."

"Court in two weeks?" Lacey turned and smiled at Jay. He was leaning against the door frame, watching her. "That soon?"

"In a situation like this, with the parent giving up her rights, the process is a little easier and definitely takes less time."

She looked away, focusing on the call, the details and the baby that would be hers. She said good-bye and hung up, knowing that Jay had moved closer, that he was behind her.

"Good news?"

She nodded as she finished putting the new diaper on Rachel. "Court in two weeks. They approved the home study."

It felt like they had approved her. She felt a little lighter, a little freer.

"Would you like me to go with you?" He took the dirty diaper she handed him and she pointed to the trash. He cringed a little and held the diaper as if she'd handed him a poisonous snake. He had delivered calves and foals, cleaned stalls, and he couldn't handle a diaper. She smiled, because he had offered to go to court with her and she wanted to forget how it had felt when Lance broke her heart.

"You don't have to go." She wiped her hands with baby wipes and picked up Rachel. How could she tell him that each time he moved a little further into her life, she thought about what it would feel like to be loved by the cowboy next door? She thought about how it would feel to watch him walk away.

She wanted to hear about Jamie, from him, not from Bailey or someone else.

"I think we should eat." She grabbed the bouncy seat for the baby and handed it to him.

"Good idea." Letting go of secrets, of wanting something she couldn't have. He hadn't told her about Jamie, and that meant something. It meant he didn't want her to share that part of his life, or know about that broken piece of his heart.

As they walked out the back door she wondered if he thought of Jamie when he visited. Was he thinking about the memory of a girl he had loved, who owned his heart?

She stopped herself, because she didn't know the story. She hadn't let Bailey share his secrets. Anything she came up with was speculation.

"You okay?" He stood under the cherry tree where she'd placed a picnic table she had bought at the local flea market. She had painted it bright yellow.

"I'm fine, just hungry. Do you want to get the food out of the fridge and I'll buckle Rachel in the bouncy seat?"

Did he want to tell her about Jamie? She bit down on her bottom lip and tried not to imagine what she read in his dark eyes. She wouldn't let her heart be broken again.

Jay turned and walked away, straight back and dark blue T-shirt. Two months ago he had been a stranger. When he came back with the picnic basket and lemonade, he still wasn't smiling.

"Lacey, we can be friends."

"I know that." She really did. She looked away, sliding the

pacifier back into Rachel's mouth, and then opening the basket that Jay had placed on the table.

He moved behind her, close. Too close.

His hands brushed her arms and he leaned, kissing her neck from behind, his hands still resting on her arms. "Turn around."

He whispered the words into her ear and she turned, aware of his cologne, aware of mint and the sweet scent of summer clover as bees buzzed. He cupped the back of her neck and his lips met hers, tasting like mint—and forever.

Lacey's mind played tricks on her, reminding her of a girl who had done things to feed her family, to keep her siblings in a home through the winter. And this cowboy, strong and sure of himself, he had never had to make those hard decisions.

She backed away, "No."

"What?"

She shook her head, feeling ridiculous for even letting herself believe in forever. "I'm a dirty sock."

He smiled just a little. "A dirty sock?"

"You're a clean sock and I'm a dirty sock. We're not a matched set. We're not…I'm not going to play games and kiss you on a summer day, believing in fairy tales and forever. I know who I am and what I am. I know that I'm not someone's forever. I'm just the girl that's easy to kiss on a summer day. I'm just a friend."

"Lacey, you have the oddest way of putting things. I'm not playing games. I don't play games."

"Then tell me about Jamie."

He backed away, looking wounded, as if she'd slapped him. "Keep the food. I have to go."

"Jay, wait. I'm sorry."

He turned and stopped. "For what? For thinking such ridiculous thoughts about yourself, or for listening to gossip?"

"I didn't gossip."

"Then how do you know about Jamie?" He took a few steps toward her and her breath caught in her lungs, hopeful, thinking he might not walk away.

If he shared, what would that mean?

"Someone tried to tell me, and I wouldn't let them."

"I don't want to talk about Jamie." .

"Okay." She bit down on her lip and told herself she wouldn't cry. She wouldn't let her heart be broken over the closed look on his face.

He hadn't shared. What did that mean?

"I'm not ready for this." He shrugged. "I'll talk to you later."

Not ready for what? She wanted to throw the question at his retreating back. Not ready for a relationship, or not ready to tell her about Jamie?

Chapter Fifteen

Lacey didn't see Jay again until Sunday. He was in his uniform, getting out of his patrol car, and she pulled into the church parking lot. He was leaning against the car parked next to hers when she opened the door of her car.

"Need some help?" He reached for the back door. "I can get Rachel."

"Oh, okay." But not really okay. Not when there was an incredible distance between them.

"You should come and see Dandelion today. I have a halter on her and she could use some attention. The more we mess with her now, the easier she'll be to handle as she gets older."

"I can do that."

"Lacey, I'm sorry about the other day. I thought I could do the picnic."

"Don't apologize, Jay. It was a mistake on both our parts. We should stick to friendship. I think we might be good at being friends."

He nodded and smiled again, but then his gaze shot past her. "I don't recognize that car."

A cop. She'd somehow forgotten that he was a cop. She

turned, wondering why a car would intrigue him. It was church, and the whole idea was for people that didn't normally come to attend. That was a good thing.

The car in question was moving too fast and the right front tire was a spare, the doughnut kind that looked like it belonged on a bike. And the woman behind the wheel was Lacey's mother.

"This can't be happening," Lacey muttered. Her heart did a painful, nervous squeeze.

"Who is it?"

"My mother." Or the woman who claimed the title. *Forgive.* The word rolled through her mind, because it was necessary to let go, and to forgive.

"I'm with you." His voice was strong, and he didn't move away from her.

He was with her. A friend. And yet he didn't share secrets. She blocked thoughts of Jamie, previously a name whispered in connection with his, but not a real person. Now she felt very real. She was living, in a surreal way, in Lacey's dream house.

Lacey's mom parked her car and got out. Deanna Gould was nearly fifty, but still tried to look like a woman in her twenties. In short skirts and tank tops, her hair dyed a brassy blond, she didn't pull off the younger look. Her makeup was garishly bright and her smile was stiff. A hard life had aged Lacey's mother.

"That's my grandchild," Deanna yelled as she approached them. "And don't think your cop friend scares me."

"I'm not here to frighten you." Jay still held the car seat that carried Rachel. Lacey stood close to him, feeling a little protected because he was near. For the moment she pushed aside the hurt she'd felt when he walked away.

"Well, I'm here to get that baby." Deanna crossed skinny arms in front of her.

"You can't take her." Lacey found her voice and her strength. "I have custody of Rachel. She's not going with you."

Movement out of the corner of her eyes. She turned and saw several people standing in the doorway of the church. Her stomach tightened with dread. Her old life had invaded Gibson.

"She's my granddaughter and you're not the good little girl you want these people to think you are."

"Maybe not, but she's with me and she's safe."

"She's my grandchild." Deanna's face crumpled and she looked ten years older. Lacey felt sorry for her.

"I'm not going to keep you from seeing her. I'm also not going to let you take her."

"I'll get a lawyer." Deanna took a few steps closer, looking as if she might really try to grab Rachel and run. Her gaze glued to the baby, and then traveled up, to Jay's face. "You can't keep me from getting her."

"We're going to court, Mom. I'm going to adopt her."

"You? With your record?" Deanna laughed, a harsh laugh.

"That was a long time ago."

"Why don't we all go into church and we can talk about this later?" Jay, calm, in control. Lacey felt like her insides were shaking as badly as her legs.

"Go in there?" Deanna looked past them, eyeing the church and looking less than sure. "Well, if it means seeing my grandchild, I guess I can."

Wonderful.

Jay touched Lacey's back. She wanted to move closer to his side. She didn't. Instead she walked a little taller, telling herself she could do this. She could walk through the doors of this church with her mother. She could face people who had become like family to her. These people who had prayed for her mom, for her brother and sister.

It had been easy, praying for a mother who lived four hours away. Having her here, walking through the doors of the church, wasn't as easy. This was reality, and it was glaringly bright, like a spotlight in the dark, shining into the corners of Lacey's past, highlighting who she had been before she came here.

Reality.

She shuddered and Jay reached for her hand. His hand was warm and strong, his fingers clasping hers. The security of his touch was undone by the look her mother shot at her, a look that accused and mocked. Lacey knew that this day changed everything.

"You must be Deanna Gould, Lacey's mother." Pastor Dan reached for Lacey's mother's hand, greeting her with a smile that was genuine. It was the smile that Lacey couldn't work up to.

"That's me." Deanna looked past him, no longer smiling, no longer looking confident.

"Welcome to Gibson, and to our church."

"Yeah, thanks." Deanna peeked through the doors into the sanctuary. "I've seen enough and I'm not going in there. Lacey, I'll be waiting in my car for you to finish up your little charade here."

"It isn't a charade, Mom."

"Oh, I think it is. Why don't you let me keep Rachel while you're in church?"

"No, she's going with me." Lacey took the baby from Jay. "You can see her later."

Deanna Gould shrugged, and with a smile, she walked away. She had always walked away when things got tough. Lacey watched from the doorway as her mom got back in her car. And instead of waiting, she started the old sedan and drove away.

For some reason, Lacey had convinced herself that her mother would be gone when she got out of church. Deanna wasn't gone. Her car was back in the parking lot, windows down. Deanna was drinking a soda and blowing smoke rings out the window.

Lacey felt the stares of people she considered friends as she crossed to her car parked next to her mother. She tried to block her imagination from telling her what people would say about her. She tried to block thoughts of dinner tables and comments about Lacey Gould.

"Hey." Bailey hurried toward her, blond hair free, skin glowing with the health of her pregnancy. "Don't run off."

"I have to go." Lacey held the seat with Rachel. What had she thought? That this would be easy? That she'd be able to take this baby and raise her with no one objecting?

"Do you want us to come with you?" Bailey glanced in Cody's direction. Her husband stood a little distance away, Meg at his side. He nodded and smiled. Friends who wouldn't let her down.

She didn't want to think about other people seeing her there with her mother, hearing her mother's accusations.

"I can handle it." Lacey smiled because she felt stronger now. She could do this. "She wants to see Rachel, that's all."

"You call if you need us." Bailey gave her a quick hug. "Don't forget that you have friends."

"How could I forget?"

Lacey buckled Rachel's seat into the back of the car and walked around to her mother's open window. Deanna Gould blew another puff of smoke and dropped her cigarette out the window. Lacey stepped on it.

"Ready to go?"

"Do you have something for lunch?" Deanna lit another cigarette.

"I put a roast on this morning. I take it you're staying?"

"Where's your Christian charity, Lacey?"

"It's here, don't worry." She pulled her keys out of her pocket. "Follow me."

"My car won't start."

Lacey resisted the urge to sigh. "You can ride with me."

The Lord won't give you more than you can handle. Pastor Dan had preached that sermon a month ago. It had been a fresh message on verses sometimes tossed around to help cover someone else's troubles. But the meaning was strong, that God would help us through whatever situations we faced. He would give us the strength and grace to make it through trials and tribulations.

God wouldn't leave us to drift alone.

He even had a plan for Deanna Gould being in Gibson. Lacey couldn't think of what the plan might be, not at that moment. Maybe it would be one of those hindsight things that she would figure out later.

Later, when she wasn't thinking how her mother's presence would rock the boat that was her life.

"Stop looking like I'm the worst news you've ever had. I think giving that baby of yours up would qualify for that. And here you are, thinking you can replace that kid with Corry's baby."

"Stop." Lacey started her car. She watched Jay's patrol car leave the parking lot, lights on. He must have gotten a call. "Stop trying to beat me down."

Her mom buckled her seat belt. "I'm not beating you down, just being honest. You are who you are, Lacey. You're not someone that a guy like that cop dates, not for real."

"Stop." Lacey pulled out of the parking lot, her foot a little heavy on the gas. "Keep this up and I'll take you back to the church and I won't let you see Rachel."

"I'll get a lawyer and make sure you don't get to adopt her."

Lacey couldn't stand to lose more. She couldn't handle the thought of losing her heart, losing the baby and losing the community that she loved. "You can't do that. I have an approved home study and Corry signed over custody."

Deanna Gould looked out the window, shrugging as if it didn't matter. "I need money to get home."

It all came back to money. Lacey didn't hold back the sigh, not this time. "I don't have a lot of money."

"I can't get home with a broken-down car and ten bucks."

"Fine, I'll give you some money. And there's a mechanic in our church who can probably get the car running. I'll buy you a used tire tomorrow, to replace the spare."

"Don't forget to let me know that you'll pray for me. Isn't that what you always say when you call? When you used to call, that is." Was that hopefulness in her mother's tone?

Lacey's heart thawed a little. "Mom, I pray for you all the time."

And someday, someday she knew God would answer those prayers. Maybe this was a start.

Lacey's car was at home. Her mom's car was still parked at the church. Jay pulled his truck down the drive and parked behind her sedan. He didn't get out. He felt as if he was tangled in a spiderweb of emotion and the more he tried to untangle, the stickier it got.

He didn't know how to be in Lacey's life, and all day he'd thought about how to walk away without either of them getting hurt.

And here he was, parked in her drive, waiting for her to come outside. He opened the door and stepped out of the truck as the front door of the house opened. He told himself he had just stopped by to check on her. People were worried. He was worried.

She was dressed in shorts and a T-shirt, her auburn-streaked hair pulled back with a headband. She smiled and wiped her hands on her pants.

"I was doing dishes." She shrugged.

"I wanted to check on you. Pastor Dan and a couple of other people called this afternoon. They were worried."

"I'm fine." She glanced over her shoulder, looking less than fine and a little worried. "Her car isn't running and I need to find a tire to replace the spare so she can go home."

"I'll go take a look at the car."

"You don't have to do that." She spoke as if he was a stranger, less than a friend. That didn't add up.

"Lacey, are you sure everything is okay here?"

She smiled then and glanced over his uniform. "I don't need police backup, Jay. I'm used to dealing with her games. She wants money to go home, to leave Rachel and me alone. I'll give her what she wants if it means an end to this."

"Don't let her manipulate you that way."

She shrugged slim shoulders and smiled a little. "You make a great hero. But really, she's not going to hurt us. And after everything she said about me today, it's better if I stick to myself for a while until this blows over."

"What does that mean?"

"It means that people will talk. I'm not the church Sunday-school teacher or the nursery worker. I'm not Lacey who works at the Hash-It-Out. I'm Lacey from St. Louis and I have a police record. I'm a fraud who sneaked into this community and pretended to be someone I'm not. And now everyone knows."

Jay brushed a hand through his hair and sighed. "Lacey, you can't believe that's true. The people here care about you. You're a part of their lives." His life. He cared. He looked away, getting his thoughts together. "And you didn't hide who you are. You told the people closest to you, and the rest didn't really need to know."

"My heart knows that. My brain only knows that my mother is here and now everyone is looking at me like I'm someone they don't know."

"It'll blow over."

"And if it doesn't blow over?"

"It will. Right now you feel like it won't, but if you think back, nothing like this lasts forever. It settles down in time. That's how a small town works."

"Thank you, Jay. I'm glad we became friends."

He nodded and walked away. Friendship. He had a lot of thinking to do. Lacey thought they had friendship, and that would have been an easy option for them both. Friendship didn't include strings. Friendship should have made walking away easy to do.

This felt anything but easy.

Lacey walked back into the house and found her mother on the sofa with Rachel, hugging the baby close. Had Deanna Gould ever held her own children that way? Lacey couldn't remember. She remembered boyfriends, drunken parties and men that she and her siblings hid from.

Lacey remembered an empty pantry and selling herself on a street corner because her siblings were cold and hungry and she had exhausted every other avenue of hope.

They had all escaped in whatever way worked for them. Lacey ran. Corry turned to drugs. Chase joined the marines when he turned eighteen.

For years she'd had nightmares of that life. Now she had dreams that included Gibson and a small house in the country. Maybe even a cowboy. Someday.

"She's a beautiful little girl." Deanna kissed Rachel's pink baby cheek. "I really messed up our lives, didn't I?"

Lacey shrugged and sat down in the easy chair across from her mom. "I don't know, Mom. I guess you did. It wasn't an easy way to grow up."

Deanna's eyes watered. "I'm not sure if I can change my life. I'm too old. I really am glad you found something better. It makes me so angry sometimes, that you chose this place over your own family, but I guess it makes you happy."

"It does make me happy. And this will be a good place to raise Rachel. She won't have to worry…"

"I know, I know. Don't accuse me, okay?"

"I'm not. Mom, I forgive you."

"I didn't do anything wrong."

Let it go. Lacey sighed. "Jay is going to look at your car."

"Are you in a hurry to get rid of me?"

"No." She knew that was a lie. "Mom, I don't mind you being here, but I don't want you to cause problems."

"I'll mess up this pretty life you've built for yourself?"

"Maybe that's what I feel. I don't know. But I won't let you have Rachel and I won't let you manipulate me."

"Lacey, I don't have a house to go back to."

Lacey wanted to cry. She wanted to hit something and scream that it wasn't fair. Her mom shouldn't be able to come here and do the same thing she'd been doing all of Lacey's life: create instability. Lacey had her life organized and settled, the way she'd craved during her childhood.

"I guess you don't want me here?"

"I don't know. We'll figure something out." Lacey stood up and reached for Rachel. "But what about you taking Rachel? What kind of game was that?"

Her mom shrugged. "I knew I couldn't take her. I guess I thought if you had money, you'd give me some to get rid of me."

"I don't have money. Corry already stole it all."

Lacey walked out the front door to the porch, Rachel cradled and protected against her chest. She heard laughter and glanced in the direction of the Blackhorse house. Wilma Black-horse stood in the yard watering her flowers, and from the way Jay jumped and ran, Wilma must have sprayed him with the water hose.

A normal family. Lacey's heart ached, empty because she wanted that space in her life filled with people that would be that for her. She wanted a family that didn't crash and burn as often as other families sat down for dinner together.

She wanted people to come home to, to share dreams with and to lean on. She didn't want to lose what she had in Gibson.

Chapter Sixteen

Lacey sat down to roll flatware in paper napkins at the end of her shift on Monday. She glanced up as Jolynn walked out of the kitchen, two cups of coffee and a plate with a slice of pie on a tray. She set the tray down on the table next to Lacey.

"Let's chat, sweetie." Jolynn scooted out the chair next to Lacey's. "We'll figure out this situation with your mom."

"I don't know if there's a solution."

"Of course there is. I haven't rented the studio. We'll put your momma there and she can do something. I'll have her wash dishes and maybe we can have her clean up around our place."

"But…"

"But you don't want her to stay in town? Lacey, stop worrying about what people will think."

"That's easier said than done. You have no idea what it was like growing up with her. Imagine her at school, talking to your teachers, or attending Christmas programs with her latest boyfriend."

"She attended?"

Lacey rolled a set of flatware in a napkin and nodded.

"She did attend."

"That must mean something."

"I guess."

Jolynn scooted the napkins and covered Lacey's hand with her own. "Lacey, everyone has dreams, even people who don't seem to. Your mom might have made wrong choices, but she had dreams. Give yourself a little credit and God a little credit. We all love you and your mom showing up isn't going to change that. Maybe this is the answer to all of your prayers for her."

"I know."

Lacey wanted to tell Jolynn about secrets and dreams. She wanted to explain that her heart wanted to let Jay in, to trust him, and she couldn't. She couldn't let herself fall in love. She couldn't expect him to look at her as anything more than a friend.

"You're still frowning. Is this about Jay Blackhorse?"

Lacey looked up. "Maybe."

"And do you love him?"

She took a bite of the pie that Jolynn had set in front of her. Chocolate pie, not her favorite, but she ate it anyway. Did she love Jay? The question made her heart ache, because she wanted to let herself love him.

"I can't love Jay. Wilma and Bill are great and they've helped me so much. Helping me is different than having Jay bring me home…"

"What in the world are you talking about?"

"I heard a few ladies talking the other day, about me living down the road from Jay, in Jamie's house. I don't even know who Jamie was, but I feel her presence every single day and I know I can't compete."

"You need to ask Jay."

"I asked and he doesn't want to talk about it. Besides, he's just a friend and he doesn't owe me explanations."

Jolynn clucked a couple of times. "Lacey, Wilma and Bill

would be blessed to have their son bring you home. You're everything a woman wants for her son. You're bright, warm and loving."

"I have a record for prostitution. I'm not the girl next door. I'm the woman that a guy takes out a few times, and then he doesn't call her anymore."

"Jay isn't Lance."

"No, and I'm not asking him to make me promises. He's a friend. I want to keep him that way."

"That might not happen." Jolynn stood and before she walked away she leaned and kissed Lacey on the top of her head. "You're a beautiful girl, Lacey, but sometimes you're a little slow when it comes to figuring things out. Give it time."

Give it time. Lacey nodded, as if she could do that.

The cowbell clanged and her mom walked through the doors. She had dyed her hair a natural shade of brown. Some things did change. Lacey smiled, because she wanted her mom to have a chance at a new life.

It wouldn't be easy, but she really did want that.

Jay drove past Lacey's house a little slower than usual. He had heard the talk in town, about her and her mom. He knew that she had to be hurting over old wounds reopened. And the comments about her living next door to him.

He hadn't responded well to those accusations. Even now his blood boiled a little when he thought about the guys at the livestock auction making jokes about her and him. He'd left, not bothering to bid on a bull his dad had been interested in. Still in his uniform, he'd parked his patrol car at the station and driven home.

Lacey's car wasn't at home. He hadn't seen her at the diner, either. He had even stopped. Jolynn had told him that Lacey had left an hour earlier. She had also let him know that Lacey had heard talk similar to what he'd heard at the auction.

When he pulled up to his parents' house, Lacey's car was there. He got out, stretching the kinks from his back. It had been a long day on the job, and a long day of hurting families.

Lacey's included.

He wanted a shower and clean clothes. He didn't see Lacey as he walked through the house. His parents had her somewhere, probably in the backyard. His mom had planned to grill pork steaks for dinner. He cringed a little. He'd picked up a burger from the concession stand at the auction because he knew about the curried pork. He wouldn't escape the leftovers.

On the way to the bathroom he glanced out the window of the sitting room. He saw Lacey and his dad walking to the barn. Probably to see the foal.

Fifteen minutes later he walked through the doors of the stable, his hair still a little damp. He had changed into a cotton shirt and shorts.

"Jay." Lacey walked out of a stall, the baby in one arm and a kitten in her other hand. "Look what we found."

"Great, the world needs more cats." He took the kitten that she held out to him. "Do you want me to put her back with the rest of the litter? Or do you want to take her home?"

"She isn't ready to be weaned." She looked up, uncertainty shadowing her eyes. "Maybe in a couple of weeks. I'd like for Rachel to have a kitten. And maybe even a puppy."

"I think we can find her a puppy." He walked into the stall and put the kitten with the others. When he walked out, Lacey was waiting. "Did you see Dandy?"

"I did. She's beautiful. Your dad helped me put a lead rope on her and she's wonderful."

"She is a beautiful little thing."

"You don't have to give her to me. I mean, she's probably going to be a great horse."

"She's going to be a great horse for you. I really don't have any use for her. I think I'll put her and the mare on the two acres next to your place. You can mess with them all you want."

"Really?" Her eyes were huge and soft brown.

At that moment, he would have given her the world. The thought took him by surprise. He had to stop for a second and refocus.

"How's your mom?" He walked to the back of the barn with her. His dad was there, saddling his gelding. "Going for a ride, Dad?"

"I thought I'd check those back fences to see if I can figure out where the cows are getting out onto Seth's place."

"Good luck. I rode the four-wheeler out there a few days ago and didn't see anything."

His dad shook his head. "It's that one Angus heifer that's causing most of the problems. For all we know, she's climbing the fence."

Jay laughed. "I kind of wondered that myself. She's going to the auction next week. I don't feel like spending all my time chasing her down."

"Sounds like a good idea. I'll still take a ride and see if I can figure where she's getting out."

Jay watched his dad ride away and then turned back to Lacey. She had her fingers through the fence and her foal had approached with cautious steps and curious ears pricked forward. He didn't repeat his question about her mom. Instead he watched as she ran her fingers along the foal's muzzle. Rachel leaned against Lacey's shoulder, wrapping tiny fingers in dark hair.

"I think my mom is moving to Gibson." Lacey turned to face him when the foal pranced away, skittish because a cat had walked out of the barn. The mare nuzzled her foal and the baby leaned into her mom and started to nurse.

Lacey's mom was staying. Jay leaned on the fence and watched the mare and foal, not Lacey.

"I wondered. Are you okay with that?" He stood next to her, and he realized that she wasn't a girl in need of someone to make her dreams come true.

"I am, but I'm not. I've prayed for her for so long, and it was easy to pray. I wanted God to send someone who would be a witness to her. I wanted it to happen in St. Louis, so that I could stay here in my safe life." She brushed a hand across her eyes. "What kind of person does that make me?"

"A person who has dealt with enough."

"Maybe." She sighed. "Let's talk about you. How was your day?"

His day. He leaned against the fence, watching the mare and foal. "We had a drug bust and it ended with two little kids being taken into protective custody. No matter how low people get, or what mistakes they make, it always rips their hearts out when you take their kids. That dad…"

Her hand was on his arm and he smiled down at her.

"It had to be hard to do." She spoke softly, encouraging. When was the last time he'd talked to someone the way he talked to her?

Never. The one word took him by surprise. Not even with Jamie. He and Jamie had shared a fantasy world that made letting go easier.

"It was," he admitted. "The parents were crying. The kids were crying."

Standing next to him, Lacey was crying. Tears trickled down her cheeks and she brushed them away. "Life without faith."

"Yes."

"Jay, I know what people are saying. I'm sorry. I'm not even sure who Jamie is, but I'm not trying to take her place. I'm sure that no one could do that. I'm the last person to try and fit into someone else's place in your life."

He nodded in the direction of the gazebo in the yard. "Let's go sit down in the shade."

"Okay."

Jay led the way, not sure what he would say, or how he would say it. He only knew that she deserved the truth. As a friend, she needed to know about Jamie.

Lacey walked up the steps into the gazebo. It was cooler there, with a ceiling fan spinning from the rafters, moving the summer air. Hummingbird feeders hung on hooks. A tiny bird buzzed past them, landing on a feeder and drinking for a long time from the nectar.

"My mom keeps the feeders full and sometimes there are dozens of hummingbirds out here." Jay sat down on a bench and Lacey sat across from him.

She wanted to sit facing him, not next to him, touching him and breathing in the scent of soap and peppermint toothpaste. But sitting across from him presented other problems. Looking at him made her think of the kiss and how it had felt when he walked away from her.

She didn't want to think about him walking away.

He stretched long, tan legs in front of him and smiled. She smiled back, but Rachel fussed against her. She turned the baby so she could look around. Immediately Rachel looked up, mesmerized by the ceiling fan.

"Lacey, I was married."

It was really hot and she was positive she hadn't heard him correctly. He had proposed and Cindy had rejected him. *Married?* She couldn't process the word.

"Lacey, are you with me?" He leaned forward, tan, lean cheeks, a mouth that smiled hesitant smiles that nearly always did something to her heart.

She took in a deep breath and nodded. "You were married?"

"To Jamie." He clasped his hands and looked up, like Rachel, at the ceiling fan. The memory she couldn't compare to. Now she understood. At least she understood a little more than she had.

"You don't have to do this. I told you, it's your story and you don't have to share." She took a shallow breath that hurt.

"I want you to know. I want you to understand. It was the summer I turned twenty. I came home from college and my mom had brought home a family. She met them in Springfield and they wanted a place in the country for the summer. She gave them the farmhouse, where you live."

"Jamie?" It was hard for Lacey to say the word, to know that he had loved someone enough to marry her.

And her heart knew that this was his way of telling her what she already knew, that she didn't belong in his life.

"Jamie. She was eighteen and a patient in the clinic where my dad works. She had six months to live and she had always dreamed of living on a farm. Mom made that dream come true for her."

"And you fell in love with her?"

He didn't answer. Not right away. His eyes were closed and he nodded. When he opened his eyes she saw his broken heart.

"I fell in love with her. She was perfect and innocent. She was full of joy and faith. She had a dream of loving someone forever. And she knew that she wouldn't have forever. So we had three months."

"Jay, I'm sorry."

He nodded and his eyes filled with tears. He didn't cry. "I promised her that I would only love her. Forever. It was all I could give."

"What about Cindy?"

"Friendship. We had a great friendship and a lot of fun together. We got tangled up in something that became a habit. It was an easy relationship that didn't require a lot from either of us. She wanted a career, and I had memories of someone else. It wasn't love and she was smart to say no when I proposed."

"I'm not sure what to say."

"You don't have to say anything. I just wanted you to know the truth, before you hear it from someone else. I wanted you to know that it wasn't about you living in that house. It isn't about who you were in St. Louis."

"That isn't true, Jay. I'll always be that girl from St. Louis. Our past makes us who we are. Remember?" Her past made her someone who couldn't compete with the memory of a perfect summer.

He didn't want anyone in that house. She understood now. She understood that he was telling her that he had already loved and lost. He had loved someone perfect, someone innocent. Someone who was nothing at all like Lacey.

She got it. She finally got it.

Our past does make us who we are. He agreed with that. That summer with Jamie had changed his life.

Lacey was looking at him, looking a little lost, looking hurt and he didn't know how to change that. He had given her the truth, it was all he had.

"I have to go now." Lacey stood, holding the baby. Rachel was still trying to look at the fan.

"Don't. You really don't have to leave."

"I know, but I can't stay."

She walked away without looking back, and without telling him she'd catch him later.

Jay stood in the gazebo and watched her go, watched her take a little of his heart with him. He didn't know how to call her back. He had never dreamed of this day, when he would want to call her back, because calling her back felt more important than holding on to a perfect summer.

He walked back to the barn, slow steps, thinking about why it had been necessary to tell her about Jamie and the promise.

His dad was back from checking fences. Jay took the reins of his dad's gelding and led the horse into the stable.

"Did you find the hole?" he asked, his back to his dad.

"I found a place with loose barbed wire. That has to be it. Not a hole, just an empty space."

Empty spaces. Jay tied the horse. Empty places that Lacey and a baby had started to fill. And that had scared the daylights out of him. It had felt like a broken promise to a girl who hadn't had a chance to live, to really dream, to be.

"What's up?" His dad pulled the saddle off the dozing horse.

"Not much."

"That's more than a *not much* look on your face."

"I guess it's a look of pretty much total confusion."

"Got a girl on your mind?" His dad handed him the saddle and reached to pick up the brush he'd brought out of the tack room.

"A girl on my mind? Dad, I'm not sixteen."

"Sorry, but I wish it was as simple as that. You're a grown man. That's hard for a dad to handle. And you're going to have to let go of something that happened when you were a kid."

"'Something that happened'?" What an easy way to characterize a marriage that had ended three months after it started.

"Jamie was a long time ago, Jay. It's time to move on and to let someone else into your life. That doesn't mean you should replace her with someone you don't love just to fill the void."

"Cindy?"

His dad shrugged. "You know the answer to that better than I do."

"I guess I do. But I made a promise to love Jamie forever."

His dad stopped brushing the horse. Jay looked away from a face so similar to his own that people often called them carbon copies. His dad hadn't known about the promise. Jay had kept that to himself, because it had seemed too private, too important.

Now it did seem like something a kid had done a long time ago.

His dad went back to brushing the horse, smooth, easy strokes. The horse twitched and stomped at flies that buzzed around his legs.

"That was a big promise to make."

"I guess it was."

"You can keep room in your heart for her and still make room for someone else. You made a promise to a dying girl. That's noble but a little unrealistic. I haven't said much over the years because I knew you'd work it out on your own."

Jay smiled at his dad. "So, why now?"

"Because I don't want you to make a mistake."

Mistake? It was up to Jay to figure that one out. Would loving Lacey be a mistake? Or would walking away from her be the mistake?

"Jay, do you care about Lacey?"

"I care about her. But I'm not sure if she's ready for a relationship any more than I am."

"I guess you've got to think about this and where you want it to go from here."

He nodded and reached for the halter of the gelding. Where to go from here? He remembered Lacey walking away. She wasn't a girl of eighteen looking for someone to fulfill her dreams. She was a woman who knew how to deal with life.

And she had walked away from him.

Chapter Seventeen

"Here you go, Mom." Lacey set the suitcase on the hide-a-bed in Jolynn's studio. "Remember, you have to work in the morning."

"I know, I know." Deanna sat down, clasping her hands at her knees. "I haven't worked in a long time, Lacey."

"You'll be fine. Show up and do what Jolynn asks you to do."

"Thank you for doing this for me. I hadn't expected you to be this good to me, not after everything I've done to you."

"I forgive you." The words were getting easier. "Are you sure you don't want to go to the rodeo with us?"

"I'll stay here and put things away. Do you want me to watch Rachel?"

Lacey shook her head. "I'm not ready for that, Mom. You have to understand that forgiving and forgetting are two different things. I can't trust you with Rachel, not yet."

"That isn't really fair. I'm not going to hurt her."

"I know." But Lacey didn't know. "I'll see you tomorrow."

She hugged her mom at the door to the apartment and she walked down the sidewalk that used to be hers, past flowers she had planted. Her place. A few months had changed everything.

She put Rachel in the car seat and buckled it, pretending

her mom wasn't at the door to the apartment, watching, wanting her to feel guilty. Someday she'd leave Rachel with her mother. Not yet.

When she drove onto the rodeo grounds, past lines of cars and trucks, she saw Jay's truck and trailer. Of course he would be there.

She parked next to Bailey's truck and got out. She turned with Rachel and saw Bailey walking across the parking area, her belly round and her top stretched tight. Lacey waved and Bailey smiled a greeting.

"I didn't know if you would come tonight." Bailey reached for Rachel. "Give me this baby girl."

"Are you sure? She's heavy."

"She really has grown." Bailey held the baby close and slipped an arm around Lacey. "How are you?"

"Good, I guess. You know people talk and you just let it go because there's nothing you can do to change the past. And talk doesn't change who I am now."

"You're finally starting to get it."

"I guess. It's easy to say. I'm working on actually feeling that confident."

"And what about Jay?"

Lacey shrugged and didn't mean to look for him. But she did. He was on his horse, a lariat in his gloved hand and his hat pulled low. Cowboy. He was a cowboy all the way.

"Lacey?"

"Bailey, I can't do this. I can't be the woman he rejects. I can't be a second-best replacement for a memory that has lived untarnished in his mind. I've worked too hard on my life to make that mistake."

"Is that what you think about him?"

"It's what I know. Now, let's go watch some cowboys rope some steers, okay?"

"You got it." Bailey sighed, like the conversation wasn't over.

They climbed the steps of the bleachers and sat midway up, away from dirt that would be flung through the fence, and close enough to see the action.

As they sat down, Bailey handed Rachel back to Lacey. She made a face and leaned a little forward.

"Bay, you okay?"

"Contraction. Don't worry, just one of those 'getting ready' kind, not the real thing."

"It looked like the real thing."

Bailey smiled. "It wasn't. Believe me, I'll let you know if it is the real thing. And then you can yell for that cowboy down there because he is not missing the birth of this child."

"I won't let him miss it."

Bailey took another deep breath and relaxed. "Court is next week. Are you ready for that?"

"I am ready. I'm a little afraid of the future, of raising her by myself."

"You'll be fine. Look at Meg down there. We managed with her, didn't we?"

Lacey smiled at Meg, sitting on the saddle in front of her daddy, her blond hair in a braid and a wide-brimmed hat on her head. The little girl waved at them.

"She's such a great kid." Lacey smiled and kissed the top of Rachel's bald little head. "Cody is a lucky guy to have the three of you."

"We're blessed. And remember the days when I didn't think that would happen?"

"I do remember."

"Remember when I was the talk of the town, coming home from Wyoming pregnant?"

"We're two different people, Bailey."

"I know that, but I'm saying to you that you shouldn't sell

yourself, God or this community short. Or that cowboy with the sweet smile and brown eyes. Don't sell him short either."

"I'm not going to do that. I'm also not going to sit and dream of something that isn't going to happen. I'm a friend. I'm someone he helps. I'm not someone he loves."

"You're still living in the past, Lacey."

"I'm all about today and the future. I'm all about raising this baby the best I can and being the best person I can be."

She held the baby close as Jay Blackhorse rode into the arena on a horse that knew every move a calf would make. Jay loosened his arm and let the lariat fly. The circle of rope dropped over the calf's neck and the horse immediately backed up as Jay dismounted and ran to the calf, flipping it and tying its hooves the way cowboys had done for centuries.

"He's pretty amazing." Bailey said the words with a tight smile. "And eventually you'll have to admit that you love him."

"I don't love him."

"Umm-hmm," was all Bailey said, and then she gasped.

"Jay, where's Cody?" Lacey's voice, screaming over the crowds. He glanced her way as he tied his horse to the back of his trailer.

"He's running bulls through the chutes. Why?"

"Baby!"

"Rachel?"

She shook her head. She had Rachel in her arms. "The baby is coming. Bailey's water broke about five minutes ago. We need to get Cody."

"I'll get him. Why don't you go back to Bailey? Get her down here to his truck."

Calm. He had to be calm and not think about babies and about Lacey five feet from him, her lips soft pink and her eyes brown and sparkling with excitement. He swallowed emotion that stuck like day-old bread.

"I'll get Bailey. Jay, it's too early." She said it so softly he nearly didn't catch the words, but when he turned, she was retreating, back to Bailey in the bleachers and a new baby on the way, too soon.

Jay hurried through the crowds and found Cody near the bulls that were penned and about to be driven into the chutes for the riders. "Buddy, you've got to come with me."

"What's up?" Cody opened a gate and waved for one of the other guys. "Let me finish this up and I'll be right there."

"Cody, Bailey's water broke."

"Water broke? Why?"

"I think it means a baby on the way."

"She's a month from her due date." Cody stood his ground, his face a mess of emotion and nerves. Meg, on the other side of the fences, started to yell for him to "cowboy up, Dad. We're gonna have a baby."

Jay laughed, because of the shock on Cody's face and the excitement of the little girl. They were making a family out of something that hadn't been a family until a short time ago. And it was working. Jay didn't want to envy, but he did.

His mind switched back to Lacey and Rachel. He didn't have time to think about promises, about Lacey. Instead he motioned for Cody to follow him.

"Cody, someone else can do this job. You're the only guy that can take Bailey to the hospital."

"I'm coming. Can you make sure someone gets my livestock home?"

"I'll get them home."

"Thanks, Jay." Cody climbed a gate and grabbed Meg. Jay watched them go, kind of wishing it was him.

"Hey, need some help?" Lacey stood behind him. He smiled and shrugged.

"I've got to get Cody's livestock home. You've got Rachel and I bet Bailey wants you at the hospital."

He wanted distance between them, because he couldn't think with her standing this close, smelling like spring. He really needed space to think.

"They took my car." She walked a little closer. "I can help you, Jay. I can drive a trailer. Bailey taught me how. I can help you get your horse home. Whatever you need me to do. There's one thing I do know, babies take time and I don't need to hurry to the hospital."

She'd had a baby. He remembered, and he knew from shadows in her eyes that she was remembering. And he saw that she wasn't letting him in, she was shutting him out.

He pushed his hat back on his head and nodded. "Okay, you can help. If you want to drive my truck and trailer home with my horse, I'll take Cody's livestock home."

"Do you want me to put your horse in the field or in a stall?"

"He's usually in the field, but it'll be easier for you to put him in a stall."

"I don't mind…"

"I know you don't, but I'd feel better if you put him in the stall. I don't want to worry about you out there in the dark."

"Okay, I'll put him in the stall. So, show me how to drive your truck."

He coughed a little. "You can't drive the truck?"

"Gotcha."

Yes, she had gotten him. He smiled a little weakly and handed her his keys. "I'll be over in a sec to put him in the trailer."

"I can do that, too."

"I know, but…"

"But he's your animal and you want to make sure. I don't blame you."

She walked away, suddenly a cowgirl and not the city girl who waited tables at the Hash-It-Out. He didn't turn away for a long second because he realized that once upon a time he had been in love with a girl.

And Lacey was a woman. She was someone a guy could count on. She didn't need a cowboy to be strong for her. She could be strong for a cowboy.

He processed that newly found knowledge because he didn't know what to do with it, or how to let go of promises he had made.

Lacey gripped the steering wheel of Jay's truck and said a lot of prayers as she drove the back roads to the farm. She had driven a truck and trailer, but this ride, this night felt different. Bailey was having a baby and Jay's horse was in her hands.

She prayed for her friend and the baby as she drove, and by the time she parked in front of the stable, her back was stiff from being tense and her jaw felt permanently clenched. She hopped down from the truck and landed on wobbly legs.

As she unloaded the horse, lights came on in the house. A door closed and someone crossed the lawn to the barn. Lacey heard Rachel's quiet whimpers in the truck and hurried to get the horse in the barn and unsaddled.

"Lacey, you okay in here?" Wilma walked up, robe flapping and hair in curlers. "Jay called. He wanted to make sure you made it."

"Worried about his horse?" The wrong words. She regretted them immediately, even if she had meant them to be funny.

"No, sweetie, he was worried about you. Let me get the baby and you put that horse in the stall. There's grain in the feed room."

"Thank you, Wilma."

"Don't mention it. It was sweet of you to do this for Jay, especially with Bailey in labor. As soon as you get finished, come up to the house. I'll give you my keys, so you don't have to drive that truck to the hospital, and I'll keep the baby."

"You don't have to do that."

"I want to." Wilma touched Lacey's arm. "Honey, we love you. I know that there has been talk and you've been hurt by that. But I want you to know, I would never be ashamed to have you as part of my family. I'm only sorry that Jay can't let go of the past and see what's in front of him now."

Lacey turned into the dark, hiding tears and choking back a sob that almost escaped. "Wilma, that means a lot to me. More than you could ever know."

"Lacey, stop telling yourself that you're the only one who has made mistakes. I made my share back in the day. As a matter of fact, I made one that nearly killed Jay's dad. But he forgave me. It wasn't easy, but we worked through our troubles and we came out stronger than ever."

"I didn't know."

"No one but Bill knew, until right now. It isn't something I'm proud of. Bill was in medical school and gone all the time. I was young and lonely and we had a neighbor that had a habit of saying all the right things. And he convinced me that Bill didn't appreciate me. Of course that wasn't true, but I was lonely and let myself believe that it was."

"I…"

"You don't know what to say." Wilma smiled as she spoke. "Pretty houses and fancy cars hide a lot of sins that we'd all rather not talk about, but we need to face and work through our sins. The Blackhorse family isn't perfect. But we're happy and we love each other. We've never pretended to be perfect. Temptation doesn't pay attention to class or location. It isn't a respecter of persons."

Wilma cleared her throat. "Now, enough of that. You have

to go see a new baby into the world. And I need to get Rachel out of the truck."

"Wilma?"

Wilma turned. "Yes, Lacey?"

"I'm glad you shared that with me."

"I am, too. I wanted you to know, you're someone I would want my son to bring home to meet his family."

As Lacey unsaddled the horse and put him away, tears flowed and she didn't try to stop them. She was good enough. Wilma wouldn't be ashamed of her. Whatever happened between Lacey and Jay, she had that knowledge and it felt good.

It felt a lot like love. It wasn't the love of a man, but the love of a family and a community. And that was enough.

Chapter Eighteen

Lacey left the hospital the next morning, blinking against the bright sunlight. Bailey had given birth two hours earlier, to a tiny little guy with dark hair and a big cry. He was small, but healthy. Lacey sighed with relief and exhaustion as she got into the car for the drive home. Back to Gibson.

She tried not to think of Jay at the hospital, and the two of them not speaking. It had felt a lot like losing a friend. And more. She hadn't expected that.

She hadn't expected silence between them.

As she drove past a new apartment complex her mind turned in a completely foreign direction. She could move to Springfield.

She could get an apartment and take college classes.

Of course that was running away. But hadn't she run away before, and it worked out for her? She had run away and ended up in Gibson.

She had found faith and love. She had found herself in that small town. And now it was all crumbling and falling apart. Her mom had invaded her life. Jay had invaded her heart.

The drive to Gibson took a little more than thirty minutes.

When she pulled up in front of the Blackhorse home, she breathed a sigh of relief because Jay's truck was gone.

As she walked up the front steps, the door opened. Wilma smiled and motioned her inside. "You look beat."

Lacey tried for a smile. "I am. It was a long night. But worth it. The baby is beautiful."

"I can't wait to meet him." Wilma motioned her inside. "And your own little angel is still sound asleep. Why don't you leave her here and go home for a nap?"

It was tempting, very tempting. The thought of sleep brought a yawn that Lacey covered with her hand. "I started to say I don't need to sleep."

"Of course you need to sleep. Unlike Jay, at least you admit that. He came home, changed into his uniform and went to work."

"He's going to be sorry." She didn't want to talk about Jay, not with his mother.

"He'll be tired tonight. Oh, that reminds me, I wanted to make sure you knew about the ladies' meeting at church tomorrow night. Will you be able to make it?"

"I might. I usually have classes on Thursdays, but since Bailey is in the hospital, I probably won't go. She usually takes care of Rachel for me."

"If you need me to take care of her, I can."

"Thank you, Wilma. But I can't keep taking advantage of you that way." She pulled her hand back from Pete, who had ambled onto the porch and nudged her. "I'm actually thinking of renting an apartment in Springfield. I realized that it would be easier for me to take classes at the university if I lived there and didn't have to spend so much time away from Rachel, driving back and forth."

"You would leave town?" Wilma frowned. "Lacey, has something happened between you and Jay?"

"No, nothing." Only moments, and moments didn't make

forever. Moments didn't equal something. Especially when the man in question was now ignoring her.

She couldn't tell Jay's mother what it felt like to be a stolen moment and nothing more. She knew she could never compare to a perfect summer, a perfect memory.

"Please don't rush into this decision. We all love you and we'd be heartbroken if you left like this. And what about your mom? Jolynn said she's doing a great job at the diner. She even accepted a dress Jolynn gave her to wear to church this Sunday."

"I know, and you're right, I won't rush."

"Go home and sleep, honey. You're just tired and things always look bad when you're tired. You probably feel like you're coming apart at the seams, with everything you've been through lately."

Lacey nodded, because if she opened her mouth to agree, she might cry. How had her perfectly structured life changed in such a short amount of time?

And in five days she would go to court to finalize the adoption of Rachel. That counted as one of the good things in her life. She didn't want to forget the good things. Everything falling into place and falling apart, all in a matter of weeks.

Nearly a week after Bailey gave birth, Jay drove down a paved country road, windows down and his radio blasting Kenny Chesney. And he couldn't stop thinking about Lacey. He wished he could go back and undo whatever had gone wrong between them. Maybe it couldn't be undone. She had been hurt by memories that he'd held on to for too long.

He hadn't been able to explain why he needed distance and time to think.

Yesterday she had told his mom that she had gone to Springfield to look at apartments. Her plans were to make a decision after her court date. He let out a sigh and gripped the wheel a little tighter. Letting go.

He drove down the road to the familiar drive that led to the cemetery. He hadn't been there in a few months. He hadn't really thought of going lately.

He was letting go. And that felt wrong. He felt guilty for the memories that were fading, becoming more a part of his past.

He stopped his truck and got out, walking up to the grave with flowers from his mom's garden. He stood for a minute staring at the headstone. *Jamie Collins. She loved to laugh.* She loved life.

For a very short time.

She wasn't buried here. Her parents had taken her home for a real funeral. This place was for Jay, to remember, to have a place to go. Her parents had bought the marker. They had insisted on keeping Jamie's last name the same.

He placed the flowers in the vase attached to the granite marker and stepped back. It was time to move on, to let someone else into his life, and into his heart. It had been time for a while now, but he realized the other day that the right person just hadn't come along.

Lacey had filled the empty spaces in his heart, spaces that even Jamie hadn't filled. It hadn't been easy to accept that.

"How do I move forward?" he whispered. But he knew the answer. Jamie had been a kid. He hadn't been much more than a kid when they married. He had loved her because she had been soft and vulnerable. She had needed him.

"Son, you move forward by letting go of the past."

Jay turned, surprised that he wasn't alone. The older man leaned on a cane and tears rolled down his wrinkled cheeks.

"I'm sorry?" Jay took a step back, facing the man that had appeared out of nowhere. But a quick glance around the cemetery and Jay saw the car a short distance away.

"You move forward by letting go. Or you miss out. I missed out." He wiped his faded blue eyes. "I lost my wife six years ago. She was the love of my life and no one could replace her. But I met this sweet gal at the seniors' center. She was a little younger than me, about sixty, and she had this laugh. I loved her laughter."

"What happened?"

"I didn't ask her out. My kids were hurt by the relationship. They thought I wasn't being loyal to their mother's memory. They didn't understand how lonely I was, and I didn't want to hurt them. So I didn't date my gal friend. We still had coffee from time to time, and occasionally we sat together, but we didn't date. And now she's gone."

"She passed away?"

"Nope, she married someone else." The older gentleman smiled and winked. "I'm really sorry I wasn't the one to marry her. Now, what's your story?"

"I promised my wife I'd love only her, forever."

"You were young, weren't you?" The older man nodded at the granite marker. "I remember being that young. You can love her forever. But make room in your heart for other people, other love and more experiences."

"I think you're right about that."

"Well, if you've got a sweet gal that you could love, I think I'd make an effort to work things out with her."

"I'm going to try, if it isn't too late."

"Unless she's married another man, it probably isn't too late. Or maybe you don't have the courage?"

Jay smiled. "I think I have the courage."

"Does she know how you feel about her?"

"No, she doesn't."

"It seems to me you need to work on relationships. Communication. They talk about that a lot on those afternoon talk shows. You might want to watch one." The older man took a few steps with his cane, leaning heavily for support.

Jay laughed at the man's comment. "Yes, I guess I probably do."

"If not with her, then with someone else."

"Thank you. I guess I needed to hear that."

"Yes, you probably did need to hear that. Sometimes our hearing takes a while to kick into gear. It was nice talking to you, Jay Blackhorse."

Jay blinked a few times and the man laughed again.

"You're wearing a name tag. You're a little jumpy, aren't you?" He held out an aging and wrinkled hand. "Gordon Parker. Maybe I'll see you around some time."

Jay watched Gordon Parker walk back to his car, and then he sat down on a nearby bench. His mind went back to that summer that Jamie entered his life. She had needed him in a way that no one else had ever needed him.

Need.

He leaned back and looked up into the green canopy of leaves above him. She had been a girl, innocent and desperate to live.

In the months of their marriage he had helped make her dreams come true. And now he was tangled in memories that had faded, but he had worked to keep alive.

Coming home had changed everything, because Lacey had shown him the difference between loving a girl and loving a woman.

He closed his eyes as he thought those words. Loving a woman. A woman he had pushed away, and who thought she wasn't good enough to be loved forever.

Jay's phone beeped, signaling a text message. He flipped it open and read a message from Bailey.

Have you forgotten what today is?

He had.

* * *

Lacey had made the decision to go to court alone. So it was her, Rachel and the attorney who walked up the courthouse steps. Bailey was at home with the new baby, and Deanna had taken Lacey's shift at the diner. She could have asked Wilma to come with her, but that would have meant possibly seeing Jay. She'd been avoiding him for the last week, trying to let go of dreams she should never have allowed to form.

Why, after all of these years, had he been the one to make her dream of forever? She didn't want to think about that, not now. Thinking about Jay brought a tight lump to her chest and tears that stung her eyes.

If she could do this alone, she could do anything. Even sign the contract for the apartment in Springfield. She could go to college and be a teacher.

"It'll all be over in less than an hour." Her attorney patted her arm in a fatherly gesture. She smiled at him, thankful that he'd taken this case and thankful that Bill Blackhorse had paid the legal fees. She didn't know how she would ever thank them for all they'd done for her.

"Will my sister be here?"

"She will."

Lacey nodded, because it was okay that Corry would be at court. They'd seen each other a few times and Lacey knew that her sister really was trying to get her act together. She was clean, because she had no other options in jail. And she was still attending the church services with the minister that visited the inmates.

The lawyer pushed the door open and motioned Lacey inside. The building was old and smelled of polished wood and history. It was the smell of a government building, or a library. Lacey blinked to adjust to the dim light.

"This way."

He pointed and she followed him to the elevator. They waited a few minutes and the doors opened. Lacey stepped inside with Rachel. The lawyer, Mr. Douglas, followed.

"Lacey, you're going to be a good mother to that child. You really need to feel good about this."

"I do." She smiled to prove it. "I do feel good about what I'm doing. It's just hard."

Because she had given up her own child. She smiled through eyes that blurred with tears because she couldn't share that with her lawyer. He knew about that other baby, that little girl. It had been brought up because it did affect the outcome of this case. She had given up a child and now she wanted to adopt one. That had to be clarified so that the ruling would go her way.

She prayed it would go her way. Her stomach tightened with thoughts of losing Rachel because the judge or the social workers, or someone, thought she might not be a suitable mother. What if they took Rachel from her today?

She couldn't lose the baby. She thought about losing, and Jay. She really couldn't lose any more, could she? But then, hadn't Job lost everything and more? And he had continued to have faith, even when it wasn't easy.

What if God wanted her to lose everything?

Her thoughts were spiraling down and she couldn't let that happen. "Mr. Douglas, would you pray for me?"

He nodded and as the elevator climbed, he prayed. The prayer didn't stop her heart from breaking.

Jay pounded the steering wheel of his truck as he cruised the overcrowded parking lot. Not an empty space in the place and he knew that the hearing started in less than ten minutes. Lacey was alone. He didn't want her to be alone.

Ever.

But if he didn't find a parking space, that was exactly what would happen. Besides that, what guarantees did he have that she would want him to be there with her?

A group of people walked across the intersection and toward a car in the parking lot. Like a vulture, he watched them get out keys and get into the car. He circled, waiting for them to back out, and praying no one else would challenge him for that spot.

The car backed out and he zoomed into the empty space with barely enough room to get his door open. As he hopped out, he reached back into the truck for the bundle of flowers he'd picked when he went home to change clothes. He smiled, a little embarrassed by the scraggly bouquet. No one but Lacey would understand.

He ran up the stairs of the courthouse and through the front doors. The courtroom was up the stairs or the elevators. There was a crowd at the elevator so he picked the stairs. He ran, taking the stairs two at a time. A few people in the stairwell slid to the side to get out of his way. He apologized and kept going.

The bailiff at the doors to the courtroom stopped him.

"Court is already in session." The uniformed officer stood in front of the door.

"I know, and I'm sorry that I'm late, but I need to be in there with Lacey Gould." Because she was adopting a little girl and he wanted to be that child's father. His heart raced in his chest and he wanted to rush the gates to get past the armed officer.

"Sorry."

"Please, I know you're not supposed to do this, but it's an adoption and I really need to be in there."

The officer looked at the bouquet, his eyes scrunching. "You're taking that in there?"

"It isn't hiding a weapon, I promise."

"No, I'm just saying, couldn't you have done better?"

"Nope, this is the best."

The officer shook his head and stepped back. "Good luck. You're going to need it."

Jay smiled and nearly laughed as he pushed the door open and stepped into the courtroom. The judge turned, staring and not happy. Jay pointed to Lacey and the judge gave a short nod.

Lacey's mouth dropped and then closed again. She smiled just a little and he held up the bouquet, wilted and more scraggly than ever. But dandelions could survive anything, and Lacey would get it.

Her smile trembled on her lips. He loved her. He had known it for a while, but now, seeing her there with Rachel and knowing that her smile was for him alone and that she was a woman who could love a man forever, he knew without a doubt that he loved her.

The judge pounded his gavel on the desk and Lacey turned away from Jay, back to the proceedings. But she couldn't stop smiling. She couldn't stop the little dance in her heart. Jay had showed up. That meant something.

Dandelions meant something.

"I see no reason for not approving this adoption," the judge decreed. He looked at Corry, in a jumpsuit and handcuffs. "I believe you've made one wise decision in a life full of unwise decisions and I hope that this is a starting place for you."

She nodded and tears trickled down her cheeks. But she didn't speak. Lacey wanted to go to her, like she had when they had been young girls hiding from their mother. She wanted to hug her sister and tell her it would be okay and they would take care of each other. But Lacey could only promise to take care of Rachel and to be there for Corry.

"Lacey Gould, this child, Rachel Gould, is now your child. Love her and protect her. Do your best to be a good mother for her." The judge took off his glasses and rubbed his eyes. "And do something about this man in my court. I think he must have something to say to you."

Lacey turned and smiled at Jay. He stood next to her, a cowboy in faded jeans. His sleeves were rolled up and he carried the most pitiful handful of dandelions she'd ever seen.

But it was the most beautiful bouquet ever. Because it was for her.

"I really hadn't planned on doing this here, with a judge and lawyers as witnesses." He held up the scraggly, wilted bouquet of yellow flowers.

"Jay?"

"Lacey, I'm so in love with you I can't sleep at night. You've filled the empty spaces in my heart and in my life. I want to be a part of your life, and a part of Rachel's life. Forever."

"Forever?"

He handed her the dandelions. "Forever. I realized the other day that you've changed my life. You're strong and beautiful and I love you."

"You love me?" Tears streamed down her cheeks, salty on her lips. She brushed them away.

"I love you."

"I love you, too."

"That's good, because it works better that way."

The judge cleared his throat. "I could marry the two of you right now and put his name on the birth certificate if you'd like."

Lacey didn't know what to say, or if she could say anything. Jay had hold of her hand and when he leaned to kiss her, she couldn't think. Because this was more than a moment. It was forever.

He kissed her for a long minute, his lips exploring hers, and his arm around her and Rachel. Lacey leaned into that kiss and his embrace, feeling safe and knowing he would protect them and cherish them.

She wasn't a replacement. She saw in his eyes and knew in that kiss that she didn't have to compete with a memory. They would make their own memories.

When he pulled away, he cupped her cheek, looking steady into her eyes. "Lacey, marry me today."

"I would love nothing more, Jay. But I think we have family and friends who might be upset with us if we didn't invite them to the wedding."

He smiled and kissed her again.

"I don't care when the wedding is," he whispered in her ear, his breath soft. "I just want to make sure you'll marry me."

"I will, but I do think we need time." She leaned into his embrace and around them people clapped. Her cheeks heated and she buried her face in his shoulder.

"You're right, Lacey, dandelions are about the most beautiful flower. They're like us. They can make it through anything."

Lacey walked out of the courtroom at his side, no longer alone. She had a family now. She had a little girl that clung to her neck and cooed happy sounds, and a cowboy that had promised to love her forever.

* * * * *

Dear Reader,

Life sometimes feels like a puzzle that isn't quite coming together the way we want it to. We have all the pieces, we know what it is supposed to look like and we know how we want it to go together, but for some reason we can't make it work.

As things crumble, as pieces fail to fit and nothing seems to work, we begin to see the edges of the puzzle come together. The framework is there, it just takes time and patience. Sometimes we have to move on and then later, when we look back, we suddenly see that what we thought was a plan falling apart was actually God's plan coming together.

Jay and Lacey, like so many of us, thought they had their lives all planned out. God had something totally different in mind and when He started to work in their lives, they first thought that things were falling apart and their own plans were coming unraveled.

Like us, Jay and Lacey had to learn to let go of what they thought would be best for them, and realize that God had something even better in mind.

I love to hear from my readers. Please visit my Web site, www.brendaminton.net, and drop me an e-mail.

Blessings,
Brenda Minton

QUESTIONS FOR DISCUSSION

1. Lacey Gould's sister shows up in Gibson and Lacey has to dig deeply for the right response to Corry's arrival. Why did she have reservations about Corry being in Gibson?

2. Lacey finds it easier to help her sister when she makes it about the baby. Why?

3. Jay Blackhorse hasn't lived in Gibson for years. Why did he find it easier to live in Springfield rather at home, around his family and friends?

4. Corry wanted to believe that Lacey's new life was a charade. Why? How does that make Lacey feel?

5. Lacey comes to Gibson looking for a fresh start, and wanting to leave her old life and the mistakes she made behind her. Does that happen? Or does she have to deal with the past in order to make the present work?

6. Jay isn't thrilled with the idea of Lacey living in his grandparents' home. But Lacey reads something into his expression and she decides it is about who she is, not realizing it is about his own life. How would the truth have changed their relationship from the beginning?

7. Lacey's sister has a learning disability. How did that change her life? Do you think it was a part of her rebellion and animosity?

8. Would Lacey have reacted differently to Corry if Corry had

appreciated her more? How does that change our reaction to people we're helping?

9. Lacey's past isn't who she is now, but it did make her the person she is. Without her life in St. Louis, her police record and escaping to Gibson, her life would have changed. Would it have been the life God wanted for her?

10. Jay and Lacey both realize that God has a plan for their lives. That plan doesn't just include where they are now, but what they've been through and who they are because of their life experiences. How does it help us to see that plan when we look back and see how things in our lives have worked out, even when it appeared situations were going to do anything but work out for the best?

11. Bailey tells Lacey that she is not a finished product. Her story is still being written. We all have dreams, things yet to be accomplished. How does God figure into those dreams, gifts and the future?

12. Jay finds it hard to let go of memories and move on. Did he make mistakes in handling his relationship with Jamie? Should he have let go sooner?

13. Lacey considers herself a "dirty sock." She doesn't believe she's the type of woman a man takes home to meet his family. How does that defeat what God has done in her life?

14. Lacey realizes she has changed her family. By becoming someone they can count on, she has become the first step in changing future generations of her family. How?

15. Jay comes to terms with his love for Lacey and realizes it is the love of a woman that he needs, not the memory of loving a girl. How do relationships change as we get older?

* * * * *

When her neighbor proposes a "practical" marriage, romantic Rene Mitchell throws the ring in his face. Fleeing Texas for Montana, Rene rides with trucker Clay Preston—and rescues an expectant mother stranded in a snowstorm. Clay doesn't believe in romance, but can Rene change his mind?

Turn the page for a sneak preview of
"A Dry Creek Wedding"
by Janet Tronstad,
one of the heartwarming stories
about wedded bliss in the new collection
SMALL-TOWN BRIDES.
Available in June 2009 from Love Inspired®.

"Never let your man go off by himself in a snowstorm," Mandy said. The inside of the truck's cab was dark except for a small light on the ceiling. "I should have stopped my Davy."

"I doubt you could have," Rene said as she opened her left arm to hug the young woman. "Not if he thought you needed help. Here, put your head on me. You may as well stretch out as much as you can until Clay gets back."

Mandy put her head on Rene's shoulder. "He's going to marry you some day, you know."

"Who?" Rene adjusted the blankets as Mandy stretched out her legs.

"A rodeo man would make a good husband," Mandy muttered as she turned slightly and arched her back.

"Clay? He doesn't even believe in love."

Well, that got Mandy's attention, Rene thought, as the younger woman looked up at her and frowned. "Really?"

Rene nodded.

"Well, you have to have love," Mandy said firmly. "Even my Davy says he loves me. It's important."

"I know." Rene wondered how her life had ever gotten so

turned around. A few days ago she thought Trace was her destiny and now she was kissing a man who would rather order up a wife from some catalog than actually fall in love. She'd felt the kiss he'd given her more deeply than she should, too. Which meant she needed to get back on track.

"I'm going to make a list," Rene said. "Of all the things I need in a husband. That's how I'll know when I find the right one."

Mandy drew in her breath. "I can help. For you, not for me. I want my Davy."

Rene looked out the side window and saw that the light was coming back to the truck. She motioned for Mandy to sit up again. She doubted Clay had found Mandy's boyfriend. She'd have to keep the young woman distracted for a little bit longer.

Clay took his hat off before he opened the door to his truck. Then he brushed his coat before climbing inside. He didn't want to scatter snow all over the women.

"Did you see him?" Mandy asked quietly from the middle of the seat.

Clay shook his head. "I'll need to come back."

"But—" Mandy protested until another pain caught her and she drew in her breath.

"It won't take long to get you to Dry Creek," Clay said as he started his truck. "Then I can come back and look some more."

Clay didn't like leaving the man out there any more than Mandy did, but it could take hours to find him, and the sooner they got Mandy comfortable and relaxed, the sooner those labor pains of hers would go away.

"I feel a lot better," Mandy said. "If you'd just go back and look some more, I'll be fine."

Clay looked at the young woman as she bit her bottom lip. Mandy was in obvious pain regardless of what she said. "You're not fine, and there's no use pretending."

Mandy gasped, half in indignation this time.

Those pains worried him, but he assumed she must know the difference between the ones she was having and ones that signaled the baby was coming. Women went to class for that kind of thing these days. She probably just needed to lie down somewhere and put her feet up.

"He's right," Rene said as she put her hand on Mandy's stomach. "Davy wouldn't want you out here. He'll tell you that when we find him. And think of the baby."

Mandy turned to look at Rene and then looked back at Clay.

"You promise you'll come back?" Mandy asked. "Right away?"

"You have my word," Clay said as he started to back up the truck.

"That should be on your list," Mandy said as she looked up at Rene. "Number one—he needs to keep his word."

Clay wondered if the two women were still talking about the baby Mandy was having. It seemed a bit premature to worry about the little guy's character, but he was glad to see that the young woman had something to occupy her mind. Maybe she had plans for her baby to grow up to be president or something.

"I don't know," Rene muttered. "We can talk about it later."

"We've got some time," Clay said. "It'll take us fifteen minutes at least to get to Dry Creek. You may as well make your list."

Mandy shifted on the seat again. "So, you think trust is important in a husband?"

"A *husband?*" Clay almost missed the turn. "You're making a list for a husband?"

"Well, not for me," Mandy said patiently. "It's Rene's list, of course."

Clay grunted. Of course.

"He should be handsome, too," Mandy added as she stretched. "But maybe not smooth, if you know what I mean. Rugged, like a man, but nice."

Clay could feel Mandy's eyes on him.

"I don't really think I need a list," Rene said so low Clay could barely hear her.

Clay didn't know why he was so annoyed that Rene was making a list. "Just don't put Trace's name on that thing."

"I'm not going to put anyone's name on it," Rene said as she sat up straighter. "And you're the one who doesn't think people should just fall in love. I'd think you would *like* a list."

Clay had to admit she had a point. He should be in favor of a list like that; it eliminated feelings. It must be all this stress that was making him short-tempered. "If you're going to have a list, you may as well make the guy rich."

That should show he was able to join into the spirit of the thing.

"There's no need to ridicule—" Rene began.

"A good job does help," Mandy interrupted solemnly. "Especially when you start having babies. I'm hoping the job in Idaho pays well. We need a lot of things to set up our home."

"You should make a list of what you need for your house," Clay said encouragingly. Maybe the women would talk about clocks and chairs instead of husbands. He'd seen enough of life to know there were no fairy-tale endings. Not in his life.

* * * * *

Will spirited Rene Mitchell change
trucker Clay Preston's mind about love?
Find out in
SMALL-TOWN BRIDES,
the heartwarming anthology from
beloved authors Janet Tronstad and Debra Clopton.
Available in June 2009 from Love Inspired®.

REQUEST YOUR FREE BOOKS!

2 FREE INSPIRATIONAL NOVELS
PLUS 2
FREE
MYSTERY GIFTS

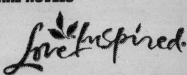

YES! Please send me 2 FREE Love Inspired® novels and my 2 FREE mystery gifts (gifts are worth about $10). After receiving them, if I don't wish to receive any more books, I can return the shipping statement marked "cancel". If I don't cancel, I will receive 4 brand-new novels every month and be billed just $4.24 per book in the U.S. or $4.74 per book in Canada, plus 25¢ shipping and handling per book and applicable taxes, if any*. That's a savings of over 20% off the cover price! I understand that accepting the 2 free books and gifts places me under no obligation to buy anything. I can always return a shipment and cancel at any time. Even if I never buy another book, the two free books and gifts are mine to keep forever.

113 IDN ERXA 313 IDN ERWX

Name	(PLEASE PRINT)

Address	Apt. #

City	State/Prov.	Zip/Postal Code

Signature (if under 18, a parent or guardian must sign)

Order online at www.LoveInspiredBooks.com

Or mail to Steeple Hill Reader Service:

IN U.S.A.: P.O. Box 1867, Buffalo, NY 14240-1867
IN CANADA: P.O. Box 609, Fort Erie, Ontario L2A 5X3

Not valid to current subscribers of Love Inspired books.

Want to try two free books from another series?
Call 1-800-873-8635 or visit www.morefreebooks.com

* Terms and prices subject to change without notice. N.Y. residents add applicable sales tax. Canadian residents will be charged applicable provincial taxes and GST. Offer not valid in Quebec. This offer is limited to one order per household. All orders subject to approval. Credit or debit balances in a customer's account(s) may be offset by any other outstanding balance owed by or to the customer. Please allow 4 to 6 weeks for delivery. Offer available while quantities last.

Your Privacy: Steeple Hill Books is committed to protecting your privacy. Our Privacy Policy is available online at www.SteepleHill.com or upon request from the Reader Service. From time to time we make our lists of customers available to reputable third parties who may have a product or service of interest to you. If you would prefer we not share your name and address, please check here. ☐

LIREG08R